Written

sweetheart.

An ANGUISHED HALLELUJAH

 BY LINDA FLAHERTY

ISBN: 1452826943

ISBN-13: 9781452826943

Library of Congress Control Number: 2010905759

To
Mother

And
In Memory Of
Mama and Papa

With special thanks to my brothers and sisters for their stories, input, and support.

I am also grateful to my son and my nephews and nieces, who responded favorably to the initial manuscript, especially my nephew and niece, Kevin Lynn Watts and Sujata Surpuriya Watts, who inspired (or was it coerced?) me to publish the collection; and to Dena, my other half, for being my lifelong tether.

Two close friends were instrumental in opening my mind to the value of childhood stories: Suzanne Keel-Eckmann was my first friend to share the unedited version of her youth, and Janet Wixson not only imparted her childhood memories but attentively listened to mine and gave them credence. My friends Mara Jambor and Lynda Wilson were kind enough to proofread the final manuscript, and Ann Flynn provided a lovely, serene space where I could edit the manuscript without interruptions.

Avery Hurt provided valuable editorial assistance. Had Fred Morris not responded enthusiastically upon reading the first few stories, I might not have completed this collection. Without the guidance of Dr. Robert McCullumsmith, I could not have retrieved, and in some cases reframed, many of the feelings associated with these memories.

CONTENTS

AUTHOR'S NOTE

These stories are factual according to my memory. The accuracy of the events chronicled in these stories has been confirmed by my siblings and our mother. They are, however, the memories of a child. The names of several of our neighbors and others have been changed to protect their privacy.

MAMA'S WORDS OF WISDOM

Mama tells me you can't make somethin' outta nothin'.

You've gotta have somethin' with which to begin.

Otherwise, you're spittin' in the wind, she says.

Like tryin' to make decent husbands outta sorry men.

Mama tells me you can't make a silk purse from a sow's ear

Or an evenin' gown from a flour sack.

She says a poor grade of fabric can't be hidden

By rows of lace or other bric-a-brac.

Mama tells me you can't make a gamecock out of a bannie hen.

That a whistlin' girl and a crowin' hen always come to some bad end.

The reference to fowl doesn't bother me 'cause I don't like hens,

But I do like whistlin', and I wonder if trouble's 'round the bend.

Mama tells me respectability is a quality not for sale,

Worth more than silver or gold, somethin' to protect.

She says your name is all you've got, and if you run it through the mud,

You'll end up like you started: fully exposed for the world to inspect.

Mama tells me not to waste time wishin' for things that don't matter a hill 'o beans.

She says many a fool's flown real high only to land in a cow paddy.

All of Mama's truisms can apply to lots of situations,

But she uses defecatin' and fallin' back in it a lot in reference to Daddy.

Funny, in spite of what she says, I watch Mama make quilt tops from scraps,

And elegant tatting from strands of thread again and again.

She makes lip-smackin' stew from yesterday's leftovers,

And cute dresses for us from the muslin sacks she buys flour in.

So I wonder, could Mama be mistaken on just this one thing,

About sows' ears, I mean, as they apply to my brothers, sisters, and me?

Could we turn out okay and to do somethin' worthwhile,

In spite of our beginnins' in shame and poverty?

Because Mama, well she sure is somethin',

And her blood flows through your veins and mine.

If we are anything like Mama,

I 'spect we'll clean up just fine.

INTRODUCTION

A stratum of Southerners has been largely omitted from most accounts of the history of the Old South. Stories of the pre-Civil-Rights South might lead the reader to conclude it consisted of genteel Southern ladies who could not pronounce the letter R (dahlin', who is yoah family?) and whose major responsibility was managing the black household servants; gentlemen who ran the local bank and mercantile, some of whom clandestinely attended weekly meetings of the KKK; African Americans whose sweat and blood made white people's lives better; white trash who were disdained by African Americans and other whites alike for their depraved and slothful lifestyles; and rednecks whose nickname connoted not the farmer's tan from which the name derived but an attitude of stubborn ignorance and prejudice.

Those stereotypes, while not totally inaccurate depictions, exclude the majority of the white rural population whose roots were also planted in Southern soil. The latter group played a pivotal role in the Old South, which should not be forgotten. These Southerners were the white counterparts to struggling African Americans, born into similar backgrounds of economic deprivation or into families that started out with some financial security but, through the colorblind hand of fate, ended up on the bottom tier, inheriting only the dream of a better life. The lifestyles of these white Southerners do not differ dramatically from that of their African American contemporaries. Like African Americans, they faced the barriers created by extreme poverty and were determined that their children's lives would be better than theirs had been. This is the story of one of those families. We are the Flahertys.

Our Flaherty ancestors lived for centuries in Ireland, on the coast of Galway. Traveling through County Galway a few years ago, it seemed to me that one of every two pubs carried our family's name. Ironically, our strand of the Flaherty clan settled in Pontotoc County, a "dry" Mississippi County where the only alcoholic beverages were brewed from corn mash as a cash crop, and the nearest legitimate tavern was one hundred miles north in Memphis. Even today, Pontotoc residents desiring a brew must drive across the Lee County line to quench their thirsts.

In the mid-nineteenth century, three O'Flaherty brothers, along with countless Irish countrymen, boarded a ship from Ireland's Galway Coast, headed for the opportunities touted in America. Our great grandfather, Hubert Alonzo Flaherty, regaled his family, in an Irish brogue, with stories from the homeland, including an allegation of how the three brothers dropped the O' in the ocean on the journey across the Atlantic. The O'Flaherty name in Gaelic means "bright ruler." According to an Irish tourism brochure written by Iain Gray, a member of the O'Flaherty lineage is reported to have created the Gaelic-Irish language by combining and refining seventy-two known languages of the time. However, the O'Flahertys were better known for the prowess displayed in battle. They seized control of the province of Connacht from the O'Connors in the eleventh century, though later the two clans united in battle against Anglo-Norman settlers who commandeered their territories. The O'Flaherty men were called the Lords of West Connacht. Stories of bloody revenge killings by the O'Flahertys abound, including the beheading of a member of the Burke clan sent to Aughnamure Castle near Oughterand, Galway, to collect rent on the O'Flaherty territory over which the Burkes had gained control. According to legend, the severed head was returned to the Burke family as O'Flaherty's rent. One member of the O'Flaherty clan is also purported to have married a female pirate, an indication that the O'Flaherty men were early proponents of equal employment opportunities.

By the time our ancestors set sail for America's land of plenty, the O'Flahertys had long since traded their swords for fishing lines and plow shares. The brothers bid farewell to their beloved island with only their personal effects and a passion for life, debate, libation, and adventure to call their own.

Eugene Flaherty, born to Hubert Alonzo and Rebecca Ida Belle, married a gentle, peace-loving, fair-skinned Etta Augusta Staten, whose good nature was passed down to their sons, Howard and Eleson, and to their daughter, Zettie Mae, but not so much to their eldest son, Olous Alonzo. Three of the four offspring inherited their father's dark Irish features, but only Olous was endowed with Eugene's headstrong, argumentative nature. With a name like Olous, he could hardly be criticized for carrying a chip on his shoulder. To his mother's chagrin, Olous changed his given name to Otis as soon as he reached legal age. In the end, Etta Augusta's wishes prevailed. Otis preceded his mother in death, leaving her to choose the monument marking his grave and the wording etched thereon. It must vex his spirit that his permanent headstone bears the name with which he was christened at birth.

On our mother's side of the family, we were endowed with our grandfather Whitworth's social consciousness and spirituality, strongly influenced by his mother's Native American ancestry. His wife, Lula Mae McCord, instilled in their children, Lowell, Louella, and Nellie, the values that had been passed down to her through her Scottish and English lineage, including the importance of cherishing your land, frugality, industriousness, ambition, and independence. Traits shared by both branches of the family tree include a strong belief in God, personal integrity, the nobility that comes from providing an honest day's work for a day's pay, a dry wit, and a level of determination that our detractors might term stubbornness.

Ours is an honorable if not aristocratic heritage, and had our father possessed a predilection toward family life or employing his above-average intellect toward achieving financial security, we could have lived quite well by the standards of the day. But then, we would not be the people we are, and I might not have one of the most loving, generous, and unconventional collection of brothers and sisters with whom one could be blessed.

These remembrances, while written about our family, tell the stories of other Mississippi families in the fifties and early sixties, as well—stories of people who, with God's grace, rose above difficult circumstances to lead prosperous lives. These recollections should live on when our memories drift upward even as our bodies sink downward into the earth we tilled.

CUPID'S FOLLY

W ho really understands one person's attraction to another? The desire to explain attraction has spawned poems, novels, and even scientific research. Scientists point to mankind's unconscious and intuitive motives in mate selection. Like lionesses, female Homo sapiens are purportedly drawn to the most virile among their pursuers. Even the way a potential mate smells enters the equation, avow proponents of the pheromone theory of attraction. Then again, those who study family dynamics contend the two could be drawn to each other because their familial dysfunctions are compatible.

A theologian friend once proffered an interesting explanation for the coupling of unlikely candidates. She suggested that somewhere in the universe, a spirit waiting to incarnate chooses the two sets of genes that will result in the desired traits for that particular incarnation on earth. My friend conjectured that the spirit's desire is strong enough to compel the would-be parents to join together. This theory is helpful when I try to fathom my parents' mate-selection criteria.

Our mother is no help at all in solving this riddle, insisting she can recall nothing about our father that should have appealed to her. Mother's remarks belie her sentiment at age fourteen when she, Nellie Whitworth, met and married Otis Flaherty, ten years her senior. The age disparity was rather common in the thirties and was not considered a perversion as it is today, but not so common was the fact that they met at a Mississippi high school they both attended. After working for a number of years, Otis had returned to school to earn his diploma. Nellie, the youngest of three children and the apple of her father's, the Reverend James "Jim" Ike Whitworth, eye, was a sophomore when they met. More puzzling than Nellie's attraction to Otis is the question: What were Jim Ike and Lula Mae thinking when they granted Otis Flaherty permission to wed their precious baby girl? Jim Ike's displeasure may be inferred, since had he been pleased, it is likely he would have performed the nuptials himself. Instead, the couple took their vows in the back seat of a car, a rather uncommon venue, which puts a new spin on the meaning of backseat trysts, and Nellie and Otis were declared man and wife by Brother Henry, a local reverend and family friend.

Nellie and Otis spent their wedding night and several subsequent months in the home of Otis' parents, Eugene and Augusta, which was located in an even more remote community than Carey Springs, the neighborhood where Nellie had grown up. Otis's father, Eugene, was a Methodist minister, but that was where the similarities between the families ended. Jim Ike and Lula Mae maintained puritanical values. Cursing, drinking, smoking, dancing, and other forms of lascivious living were prohibited. The Missionary Baptist religion dictated that these worldly temptations be overcome through prayer and supplication. The Flahertys were not party animals, but Eugene rolled cigarettes filled with Country Gentleman tobacco, and a curse word was occasionally spoken in the household. Etta Augusta was quite content to sit, dip snuff on a twig lodged in the corner of her mouth, and visit with whomever was available. She was not a friend of physical exertion. Consequently, while her house was not dirty, it would not have passed Lula Mae's test of maintaining a floor clean enough on which to serve a meal. To Nellie, the more laid-back nature of the Irish seemed slothful when compared to the stringent Scottish and English work ethic of her family.

Nellie immediately recognized her mistake. Although she loved Otis, she was yet a child, and very quickly became a homesick one. Her revelation came too late. Nellie's fate was sealed. Baptist doctrine of that era held that just as once you were saved by believing in Jesus Christ, you were always saved, once you were married by a minister, you were eternally married, even beyond the grave in your mansion in the sky. In spite of the New Testament teaching that the only unpardonable sin is blasphemy, divorce was considered unforgivable, and in Pontotoc County, no one had heard of an annulment.

This is where my theologian friend's theory gains credibility. It seems there was a long line of spirits waiting for Nellie and Otis' genes to be united. When she was sixteen, Nellie gave birth to a baby girl, Sherrill Ann, followed two years later by the first boy, Bobby Keith, two years subsequently by James Howard, and on and on at similar intervals through Larry Kenneth, Paule' Dianne (whom I christened Dena with one of my first words), and me, Linda Louetta. Perhaps the five-year delay between my birth and Betty Jo (BJ)'s signaled a decline in Otis and Nellie's popularity among earth-bound spirits. Anthony Wayne (Tony) arrived two years behind BJ, and Cynthia Nell (Cindy) appeared just one year and six months after Tony.

In fairness, there were a number of traits to recommend either of our parents individually. It was the joining of the two that was problematic. Nellie was a smart, pretty, brown-eyed brunette with a nice build. Otis was a handsome, dark Irishman, with an intellect too high for someone of his impatient and unfocused disposition. Their similar passionate natures are demonstrated by how prolific they were in creating heirs. Education held a high place on both Nellie and Otis's list of priorities. A teacher as well as a preacher, Jim Ike had stressed education as the way to improve his children's lives. He so expertly tutored Nellie as a preschooler that she entered school as a third grader. Otis's return to obtain a high school degree in his mid-twenties demonstrates the premium he placed on earning a high school diploma. Sadly, this seems to be where the couple's compatibility ended.

Lula Mae and Jim Ike had taught Nellie from early childhood that industry was a godly trait, and that cleanliness and pride in one's name were right up there next to godliness. Lula Mae had an iron will, and while Jim Ike steered the broader course of their lives, in matters of daily living, the family marched to the beat of Lula's drum. Nellie was endowed with her mother's predilection for establishing the household protocol for those around her, but she accomplished her objective in an indirect manner. So quietly did she steer the course that one could easily fail to notice who the puppet master was. Otis was given to moodiness, and could be alternately witty, withdrawn, ironic, arrogant, demeaning, and angry within any given hour. He lived to argue, and the subject being debated or the position his opponent was taking mattered very little to him. He could argue either side of an issue with equal vehemence. Nellie also had noteworthy shifts in mood, although her various dispositions presented as peaceful, joyful, frustrated or distraught. She rarely argued, but her silence and behind-the-scene manipulation proved to be quite effective in altering others' behaviors. Everyone's, that is, except Otis', and he was going to do whatever he damned well pleased and be the boss of his domain.

Nellie's vision of marriage was similar to the one in which she had grown up: a God-fearing home and a husband who returned with a paycheck each week. Otis had the ability to be a good provider for his family. He certainly could always find a well-paying job, though his pride and his quick temper made it difficult to keep one. When things did not go his way at work, he would walk off the job with no apparent thought of those depending on him for their livelihoods. Otis' idea of marriage was one that allowed him a great deal of independence and freedom.

To give Otis his due, he had a colorful personality. Among his co-workers, humorous stories of his shenanigans became legend. One of the favorites passed down to Bobby and James when they joined the sheet metal trade involved Otis and another employee installing ductwork in the rafters of a building. The foreman walked beneath them and suggested the two workers use caution. Otis thanked him for his concern, assuring the foreman he had no intention of being smeared on the floor. The foreman responded, probably in jest, that he was worried about the floor and not Otis or his co-worker. After pondering this statement for a few minutes, Otis became incensed, climbed down the ladder, packed up his tools, and walked off the job.

Otis was working quite diligently at another site, when the foreman spotted the cigarette stuck behind Daddy's ear. The foreman came by and chided, "Flaherty, we don't allow smoking on the job."

Otis retorted, "I'm not smoking."

Otis's attitude didn't go over very well with the foreman, and he replied, "You've got a cigarette stuck behind your ear."

Otis looked the foreman in the eye and said, "Yeah, well, I've got an asshole, too, but I'm not crapping." His employment ended rather abruptly.

When altercations resulted in unemployment, Otis would leave Memphis and return to Randolph, a small community in Pontotoc County where Nellie and their children resided, for a few weeks or months, explaining to Nellie that the union had called yet another strike. The news media was virtually non-existent in rural Mississippi, so his deceit went undiscovered. It did not seem odd to us that the Sheet Metal Workers Union struck arbitrarily, sometimes several times a year. As an adult, it came as a shock to learn that strikes are generally reserved for negotiation periods at the termination of a contract, occurring every few years rather than at six-month intervals.

Nellie's compulsive nature dictated that she maintain the household and family in an orderly fashion. Her challenge was Otis, who was noncompliant. He was irresponsible in matters that were not job-related. Though not as industrious as Nellie, Otis was more imaginative, and he had dreams of myriad enterprises that, if properly financed, would be lucrative while requiring little effort on his part. His imagination was especially active during "strikes," since he had plenty of time to ruminate about how his full potential as a businessman was not being tapped. The problem was the same for each of his would-be ventures—that goldarned initial investment. During one of these brainstorming sessions, Otis decided to buy a service station and to delegate its operation to Bobby and James, who were still in their early teens. It did not strike Daddy as noteworthy that neither son had any experience operating a service station, or any other establishment for that matter. As soon as his mother arrived for her next visit, he hit her up for a three thousand dollar loan so that he could purchase the service station. Etta Augusta showed good business acumen when she turned him down. After her youngest son, Eleson, was killed in Normandy during World War II, she received a government subsidy and had saved a small nest egg. Still, three thousand dollars was a considerable sum of money in the fifties. When his mother refused to finance the purchase, Otis would not speak to her for the remainder of her three-week visit. In response, she took her meals in another part of the house so that she would not have to sit at the table with him. It is difficult to ignore another person when you are living in a four-room, seven-hundred-square-foot house, but somehow they managed, leaving Nellie's nerves in shambles.

One of Nellie's compulsions was planning. Everything and everyone had to operate on a schedule, and that required considerable forethought and discipline. When a man who dislikes responsibility fathers nine children, it is a pretty good indication that planning ahead is not one of his strong suits. This deficiency was nowhere more apparent than in our family outings, which may account for their infrequency. Those occasional departures from home, touted by Otis as great fun in the offing, were predictable disasters. A particularly memorable fiasco took place one Fourth of July. An annual highlight for Nellie and her kids was her family's annual July Fourth gathering, celebrated under the huge oak tree in Jim Ike and Lula Mae's pasture. While the adults prepared the dinner, the midday meal, we played in the nearby gullies, sliding down hills until the seats of our pants were as red as the dirt. After lunch, a couple of the kids would sit atop two hand-cranked ice cream freezers while Nellie's brother, Lowell, and her brother-in-law, Sam, turned the cranks, freezing as many as ten containers before the celebration ended.

In spite of the affinity Nellie and her children felt for this tradition, the relationship between Otis and his in-laws was sufficiently strained to compel him to seek alternative July Fourth activities. On this particular Fourth, he instructed Nellie to pack a lunch and announced that the family was going to Wall Doxey State Park for a picnic. It was to be, he said, the family's best Fourth yet. At nine o'clock that morning, the Flaherty brood jammed into the car, a bunch of kids distraught about missing homemade ice cream. Undeterred by the absence of a map or specific knowledge about how to get to the planned destination, Otis confidently drove the family in a northeasterly direction. After several hours of cruising the highways and byways of north Mississippi while readjusting the glasses on his nose every few minutes, a tic that increased when he was anxious, Otis pulled off the road and announced that the family was going to enjoy a picnic on a ditch bank. The Flaherty clan returned to Randolph at four that afternoon, sweaty from riding all day in ninety degree heat with ventilation provided from the hot air coming in through the open windows, worn out and dejected, never having found the elusive Wall Doxey State Park. Not even an ice cream cone had been proffered to assuage the disappointment.

Just as with the poorly planned family outings, once Otis decided to do something, there was no stopping or delaying his action. Take, for example, the morning he received the check for his share of the inheritance from his father's estate. As soon as the check arrived that Saturday, Otis hastily loaded the family in the car and made a beeline for the nearest bank twelve miles north in Pontotoc. The banking official informed Otis he could not cash the check without his mother's signature. By this time, it was half past ten in the morning, and the bank closed at noon on Saturdays. Otis jumped back into the car, threw the gear shift located on the steering column into first gear, floor-boarded the accelerator, and headed back to Randolph to obtain the necessary signature. It was imperative to Otis that he cash the check that day rather than waiting until the following Monday morning.

Everything went swimmingly for the first few miles, un-til, as luck would have it, several miles outside the city lim-its, Otis came upon a funeral procession traveling slowly. In those days and still to a certain extent in the rural South, as a demonstration of respect, other motorists pulled off the highway until a funeral procession passed. Otis had nei-ther the time nor patience for niceties that day, his desire to return to Pontotoc before the bank closed for the day being his overarching concern. To Nellie's mortification, he began to pass the cars in the funeral procession one by one. He had overtaken a number of cars when Nellie and her children turned and looked out the back window into the faces of the riders in the car behind them: the deceased man's family members. In the front seat sat the widow, wide-eyed, stunned to see a car between their automobile and the hearse carrying her husband's body. If that was not bad enough, the bereaved widow into whose face we stared belonged to our next-door neighbor's mother. Beside her was our bewildered neighbor and grieving daughter, Fadrel—and driving the car, Fadrel's husband and our landlord, Obie. Mortified, Nellie lambasted Otis for his disregard of etiquette. To give him his due, Otis did not intend to separate the hearse from the grieving family for very long, as he soon indicated by putting his left arm out the window to signal his desire to pass that vehicle. Before he could swing our car around the hearse, the caravan reached a Y in the road, and the funeral procession proceeded right while we hightailed it to the left.

Nellie and Otis's trail of years, tears, children and jobs took them to Memphis when Bobby, James, and Larry were small, to Mobile, Alabama, in 1942 where Otis worked in the shipyards until the war ended, and then brought Nellie back to Carey Springs after she contracted tuberculosis while pregnant with Dena. Otis soon moved back to Memphis, where he lived and worked until he died, excluding a small stint in Dallas, where he took refuge to escape the authorities intent upon extracting child support from him. For the first ten or twelve years after he returned to Memphis, Otis visited the family on weekends. Nellie and her children spent the next twenty years in Randolph proper, the setting for the stories in this collection. The family owes much of its colorfulness to Otis—who was never bound by any expectations except his own—and its motivation to achieve to Nellie, Jim Ike, and Lula Mae, who gave no indication that quitting was an option.

In addition to living in interesting times, as the old adage wishes us, it is providential to be born into an interesting family. So thank you, cupid, for your folly and your genius!

LONG ROWS

A cotton row stretches for miles when viewed from three to four feet above ground. Preening on tiptoes, my sister, Dena, and I fervently searched the distant horizon for signs of stalks giving way to trees. Dena, three years my senior and a full foot taller, had a better view than me, which probably accounts for the dimmer perspective she brought to the surveillance detail.

Uncle Howard, whose cotton we were employed to pick, would set the goal of finishing the row we were picking before we quit for "dinner thirty" or "quittin' thirty," phrases he had coined for the midday and end-of-day breaks in labor. Once the end of a row was in sight, our hands took on a pattern of their own, picking at a speed we could not otherwise have enticed them to attain. Those whose hands were more adept at the task reached the end of their rows first, then turned back down the laggards' rows and picked toward them so that no time was wasted.

The end of the row was also often used as a marker for how long I could refrain from talking when the potential reward for silence was a quarter. In those days, my hands were connected to my mouth, so the faster I picked, the faster I talked, and vice versa. Aunt Carrie was the benefactor on whom I bestowed the treasures of my heart through the words that flowed from my mouth like a river, from waking until sleeping. She and I picked alongside each other in their cotton fields in Yocana (pronounced Yoc Knee) Bottom. When the eruption from my lips threatened to shatter her last nerve, Aunt Carrie would suggest to Uncle Howard that she thought he might offer a reward of immense value, one quarter, to the ones who could pick to the end of the row without uttering a sound. In truth, my vow of silence, made with such fervor, was always broken before the row ran out. It wasn't for want of trying. It was just that some amazing insight would spring to my mind, an epiphany that simply must be shared without delay, lest the world languish in darkness for even a few seconds more. Quickly, the peaceful interlude Aunt Carrie had ransomed was broken. In truth, I sometimes simply forgot we were on a mission of silence before we reached the row's elusive end.

If the truth were told, Aunt Carrie was the real culprit, and one could say she brought all the chatter down upon herself. Oh! The stories that woman could tell when appropriately prodded. Long, slow stories that took you through

all the byways before arriving at their destination, punctuated by the rhythmic popping of her Wrigley's Spearmint
gum, a skill that can be cultivated only through years of
patient practice. To be popped properly, the gum must
be flattened between the molars and rolled onto itself to
form a small bubble just before the upper and lower jaw
teeth come back together with controlled force. She was
one of the few people with the ability to take gum popping from an indication of poor rearing to an art form that
garnered respect.

The antics of Aunt Carrie's twin grandsons, Ronald and
Donald, Tenny Ruth's kids, provided fun fare, but hearing about our cousin Jane's job at Union Planters Bank in
Memphis, Tennessee, and her life as a single woman in the
big city, was hard to top for country girls who could hardly
wait to obtain from our neighbor week-old editions of
Memphis's newspaper, the *Commercial Appeal*, in order to
check out the latest romances of the girls in the *Apartment
3G* comic strip. We figured Tommie, Luanne, and Margo
had nothing on Cousin Jane. The behind-the-scenes life,
highly-exaggerated by our imaginations, we ascribed to
Jane began where Aunt Carrie's stories concluded. Jane
and our older sister, Ann, who worked in Clarksdale as a
checker for Kroger, were symbols of modern women, one

single and one married, both competing in a man's world. Then there was Glenda, the beauty of Aunt Carrie's three girls, who married a handsome guy and produced pretty babies. It was difficult to choose the family member we wanted most to emulate.

Everything about Aunt Carrie was fascinating, because she made it so. She regaled us with stories of her new shower, a convenience Uncle Howard rigged outside their house utilizing the sun's rays as a heating element long before solar energy was in vogue. He built a small square enclosure out of wood and clear plastic sheeting and placed water drums with spigots on top of the structure. Every morning before heading to the cotton fields, Uncle Howard filled the drums with water from the deep well behind their house. During the warm autumn afternoons, the same sunshine that beat down on us heated the water for Aunt Carrie's shower. At night, she stepped inside the enclosure and grasped the pulley that extended from the barrels, and down rained a warm, soothing elixir for her tired muscles. She described it in terms that allowed me to feel myself basking beneath the water's flow and to be refreshed by the mental picture her description evoked. As sundown approached, Aunt Carrie would begin her refrain about the heated bath that awaited her, requiring no effort on her part. We, on the other hand, would have to draw several buckets of water from the well behind our house and tote them inside for Mother to heat on the stove before we could remove the brown ringlets that had formed around our necks and under our arms from sweat mixed with dirt. But this was only after we had carried inside two buckets of water to clean the supper dishes from the hot meal our mother prepared after working in the fields since sunup. Uncle Howard's automatic hot water was, indeed, a fine invention. It impressed us almost as much as the indoor bathroom he installed a few years later.

Our days were long and the end was difficult to see, especially when the sun was just rising over the white fields glistening with an early frost. Sometimes, as the autumn mornings grew colder, Mother encouraged us to sit in the cab of Uncle Howard's blue pickup truck until the sun climbed above the trees and the icy coating had melted from the stalks. I did not cotton to that suggestion very much. Although the bolls were cold and stung the cuts around the cuticles inflicted by cotton burrs on previous days, and the leaves on the stalks slapped icy cold water on our faces and clothing, it was the first sack of the day that made the difference between a paltry 150-pound day and a triumphant 200-pound day. The pay was piecemeal,

3 cents a pound for the first picking, 3.5 cents for the second, and 4 cents for the third. With each picking it became more difficult to attain the 200 pounds goal. Some strapping men could pick 300 pounds a day, or so it was rumored, although I never picked with anyone who exceeded 250 pounds on a daily basis. It was only by picking with both hands at a fast clip that even 200 pounds was possible, a skill and a rhythm I mastered early, enhanced by the motor attached to my mouth. Dena was never able to achieve the two-handed picking style, probably because she did not talk fast enough. The first sack of the day, damp from dew or frost, weighed more than the others, and by the time I was twelve years old, the iron scale on the back of the truck often tipped sixty-five pounds when my sack was weighted. I waited in anticipation as Uncle Howard placed the loop at the end of the sack and the strap at the top to the hook on the bottom of the scale. It was worth the struggle of dragging the sack or lifting it over my shoulder and lumbering under the load down a long row to the truck just to see Uncle Howard edge the iron weight farther and farther to the right along the scale's metal bar.

In the grand scheme of those autumn days and weeks, to Dena and me, the amount of cotton we picked was relevant only in terms of the purchases our wages would finance. Every night after we finished the dishes and our baths, and just before falling onto our feather mattress supported by a coiled metal springs and iron frame and headboard, Dena and I would peruse yet again the Sears and Roebuck catalog to reassess our selections. Intuitively, or because of colors selected for us at young ages, we each knew the colors that were best for us. Dena, with her dark brown eyes, brown hair, and slightly olive complexion, chose browns, beiges, and greens, while I selected brightly colored fashions that accentuated my blonde hair and green eyes. The following day, as the rows loomed far ahead of us, I would describe to Aunt Carrie in exacting detail the colors, styles, and fabrics of the fashions I would proudly model for our classmates at school when classes resumed on November first.

The split school term, with classes running from July 1 to August 31 and breaking from September until November, was designed to benefit local farmers. Most children worked during those months harvesting the cotton and corn crops from our red dirt hill country just north of the Mississippi Delta. It served another purpose for Dena and me, in that we were afforded not just our summer debut of a small wardrobe acquired from the proceeds of chopping cotton and our grandmother's sewing skills, but an infinitely more impressive fall showing given the larger pool of funds available for our purchases.

Looking back on those days, I search in vain for any conversation in which Mother participated. Yet her presence looms large. Mother's day began long before ours, evidenced by the biscuits and chocolate syrup that were on the table and the potted meat sandwiches or cans of Vienna (pronounced Vi̱ Enna) sausages packed in lunch sacks, along with the Little Debbie raisin cakes or Hostess Twinkies, when she called us from our beds. Considering that Uncle Howard's blue Ford arrived before sunup to transport us to the fields, Mother's feet must have hit the cold linoleum floors by 4:00 a.m., not to be relieved of her weight until after nine each night. She picked in silence all day, apparently not needing to engage in dialog, even during dinner-thirty.

Lunchtime was a highlight, not only because we were hungry, but for the social exchange it provided. Our cotton sacks, still filled with the second picking of the morning, were dragged into a circle under a shade tree. After retrieving the lunches and sweet tea from the cab of the truck, we plopped down on our soft sacks and relished the food mother had prepared that morning. Mother dined silently while the rest of us talked and laughed as we ate. She occasionally raised an amused eyebrow when, in response to our endless marveling at Aunt Carrie's use of a whole banana on a single peanut butter sandwich compared with our practice of stretching one banana sufficiently to make three sandwiches, Aunt Carrie explained that she was conserving bread. Mother was quiet during the ride into the field each morning, and from our position on top of the cotton in the truck's bed, she didn't appear to engage in conversation with Uncle Howard on the blessed ride out of Yocana Bottom at night.

After we ate our lunches, the adults rested, and Dena, BJ, Tony, and I explored. We found Maypops and broke them open to suck the sweet, gray pulp surrounding the seeds before competing to see who could spit the seeds the longest distance. The beautiful butterflies that dined on the Maypops' flowers were fair game for chasing. Among the trees, there were Muscadine vines to swing from until, when summoned to return to the field, we declared ourselves in need of a rest. That option was off the table. In fact, our makeshift tables were already being dragged to the truck so they could be emptied.

The ride into the cotton field and the ride out were two vastly different experiences. Going in, we huddled in the cab, stacked in each other's laps, hoping to steal just one more wink of sleep. The glitter on the hay in a neighbor's pasture was a foreboding sight, signaling that Uncle Howard's field lay just ahead. As we rounded the last bend, the dew of early autumn or the frost of late fall on the cotton sparkled like rough diamonds. It was difficult to appreciate the beauty our eyes beheld with a long day's work ahead of us. The ride out of Yocana Bottom remains at the top of my favorite childhood memories. Just before dark, Uncle Howard weighed the last sack of the day, emptied it on top of the cotton already in the truck's bed, and took the iron scales down from their perch behind the truck and placed them and the empty sacks in a corner of the truck's bed. The kids scaled the ladder-like sides of the bed's railings and flopped down onto the warmth and softness of several hundred pounds of freshly harvested cotton. Snuggling down into the cotton against the chill of the early evening air, with only our heads visible, we were gently rocked over the ruts on the field road and the swish of the gravel road that took us out of Yocana Bottom, tired and sore from ten or eleven hours of labor. Along the way, the smell of supper on the stove wafted up to us from Lamar Lindsey's house, and the smell of wood burning in a cook stove in a neighbor's house made us homesick for the warmth of our home back in the days when Mother had been waiting there for us, with a fire going and supper cooked—in those better days before Daddy left us for good. We lay on our backs and watched the stars and the moon become distant objects in a darkening sky. And we dreamed quietly of future days and future places where those stars would lead us. During that half-hour ride, we forgot the toils of our day and the work that lay ahead, as we rode as princes and princesses on a white bed of infinite possibilities.

Speaking of possibilities, when it came to identifying them, no one could hold a candle to our youngest brother, Tony. Seven years my junior, he was caught right between two girls, Cindy and Betty Jo, and after Bobby and James took jobs in Memphis, he was surrounded by a household comprised of women. These circumstances may have been the impetus for his continual escape from the daily grind and his propensity to seek ways to strike it rich in a less mundane fashion. At least once a day, someone would discover Tony's cotton sack, abandoned and empty, lying in the furrow between two unpicked rows. We pondered what strange object he would bring back to the field upon his return, claiming it as his treasure. One day, Tony declared a rusted International Farmall tractor in an adjacent field that belonged to a neighboring family to be his for the taking, and he badgered Uncle Howard to haul it home behind his Ford pickup truck. He planned to restore it and get it into running condition, portending his ability in adulthood to bring almost any piece of automotive junk back to life. Uncle Howard laughingly refused to comply with Tony's wishes.

My personal favorite of Tony's antics is the time he picked clean the pumpkin patch belonging to the International tractor's owner. He was waiting for us at day's end on the side of the field road standing next to a massive pile of pumpkins he insisted Uncle Howard transport to Randolph so that he could sell them. Uncle Howard declined, not wishing to contribute to the delinquency of a youth and likely not wanting to be arrested for stealing the neighbor's pumpkin crop. You might say that Tony's problem with boundaries was apparent even at the tender age of five and that we should not so readily have accepted his deviant behavior. Nonetheless, all these years later, I chuckle when the vision of our skinny, tow-headed brother standing proudly beside that mountain of orange spheres, crosses my mind. Equally memorable were the shocked expression on Uncle Howard's face and an unusual sound: my mother's laughter.

As much fun as it sounds like we had on these daily excursions into the lowlands, it is difficult to explain why on the way to the field, Dena, BJ, Tony, and I routinely searched the skies for shreds of clouds that might collide to produce a storm. Workdays cancelled due to rain were the best of all, especially if the rain fell early enough and hard enough to ensure the cotton was too soaked to pick until the following day. Occasionally, a hurricane in the Gulf of Mexico produced torrential rains that kept us out of the field for days, and once for an entire week. The downside of those lengthy reprieves was that the blowing rain pounded the cotton into the burrs, making it difficult to pick when the water subsided. We were not forward thinking enough for this potential outcome to curtail our daily rain dances.

In retrospect, it is clear we were simply not innovative enough to produce our own work stoppage, and that we should have taken lessons from our older brothers, Bobby and James. Had we been more like them, we might have relied less upon Mother Nature and more on our own devices to control our destiny. James and Bobby, already living in Memphis by the time Dena and I were of an age to become co-conspirators, were more creative. My mother recounts a story of her young boys arriving from the fields at noontime one crisp autumn day, bedraggled and forlorn by the events that had propelled them homeward on foot. They appeared to be devastated by the loss of their lunches to wild dogs that had invaded the truck's cab through its open windows. Mother prepared another lunch for her boys and watched as they ate in a lackluster manner. She attributed their diminished appetites to the horror of having had their lunches devoured by wild animals. When she suggested they rest, they readily agreed. As they relaxed, the two boys listened avidly to the Magnavox radio as it broadcasted the final game of the World Series, a playoff between Bobby's favorite baseball team, the New York Yankees, and James' favorite, the Brooklyn Dodgers. Years later, when they were settled in lives outside Mother's home, the truth emerged. Bobby and James had eaten their lunches and contrived the story about the wild canines so they could hear the play-by-play commentary of the final World Series ballgame.

BJ had no interest in the finery advertised on the pages of the Sears and Roebuck catalog. A tomboy by nature, she much preferred to don a flannel shirt and corduroy pants on winter days. Nor did she care to pick pumpkins. She did, however, find something to motivate her during cotton-picking season. Quiet and virtually invisible, she would routinely appear perched on Uncle Howard's knee, proudly steering the Massey Ferguson tractor that Uncle Howard called Sputnik. Whenever the tractor was cranked, you could count on Betty Jo to be in the driver's seat with a broad grin crinkling her freckled nose. Her adult obsession with riding lawn mowers is hardly surprising.

Even BJ and Tony remained in the fields on the days that Uncle Howard took a bale of cotton to the gin in Randolph. When Uncle Howard took cotton to the gin, he returned with an empty truck bed and a paper sack full of cold drinks, the name by which we referred to sodas in those days. No matter what time of day he returned, we dropped our cotton sacks and scurried to the truck, inhaled the cold beverages, and burped all the way back to the place we had shed our burdens.

Only our brother Larry, away for ten months each year at the Mississippi State School for the Deaf, and our baby sister, Cindy, were relieved of field duty. On Monday mornings, we left Cindy at Mama and Papa's house, and we picked her up on Friday nights. Actually, it was on one of our rides into the fields that we heralded Cindy's birth and learned she'd been christened Cynthia Nell. At last a child was named for our mother and she could stop producing

more siblings! There is some disagreement about the deri-
vation of other names, but apparently James and Bobby
named Betty Jo after a neighbor, and Dena was named
Paule' Dianne because Mother liked the French version
of Paula. I was named for both grandmothers and Aunt
Lynda Merle, taking care of all obligations toward female
relatives in one fell swoop without proper consideration
of the fact that Louetta was not a middle name to which a
girl would ever admit. Fortunately, ours is not one of those
Southern families that insist on being called by both given
names. It is my recollection that we named Tony, formally
Anthony Wayne, after a TV benefactor who gave away mil-
lion dollar checks to deserving poor people, but Mother
says I dreamed that up.

The outside world was going through major changes
during the fifties and early sixties while ours remained
largely unchanged. We heard from Uncle Howard about
the Russian rocket named *Sputnik*, (a name he obviously
embraced since he subsequently bestowed it upon his
beloved tractor) challenging the United States in the space
race. He was intrigued by President Kennedy's vision of
landing a man on the moon. It all sounded otherworldly
to us. Through Uncle Howard's monologue, we followed
the boxing career of a man named Cassius Clay. In 1963,

the airspace over our heads was filled with helicopters and planes, as the National Guard was activated to ensure that James Meredith gained admittance to Ole Miss, just twenty miles away from us as the crow flies. That event could just as well have been occurring in South Africa. To us, it was a foreign happening, though a bit exciting because it made Governor Ross Barnett, and by association all of Mississippi, newsworthy. Only later would we understand the significance of that fall's activity and its impact on the South and even the nation. As we became more aware, some of us would admire the courage it took for a young African American man to stand against the traditions of the Old South. At the time, we did not see the Southern traditions quickly giving way to the future. In fact, it would be only a few years before our hands would not be needed to harvest Uncle Howard's cotton, as the last of the farmers succumbed to mechanical cotton pickers, which picked faster and cheaper, if not cleaner. At the time, we could not envision any of this. The cotton was too tall for us to see the end of the row.

Like other tours of duty that transport participants into remote settings from which there is no escape and subject them to grueling yet joyful experiences, those days in Yocana Bottom produced emotional bonds that will never be broken. Like the beggar's lice that, once attached to our clothes and cotton sacks, were there for posterity, such is the glue that binds our family together. Much as the burrs pricked our cuticles and made them bleed, from time to time our siblings and our mother pierce our psyches in painful ways. Just as when picking in high cotton, sometimes we have not been able to see the end of a long row. About the time we are ready to give up, lie down on our sacks, and go to sleep, a brother, sister, or our mother reaches out to us as if from an adjacent row, calling to remind us we are not alone and to provide the encouragement we need to keep going. Their words remind us that a soft, warm ride under a blanket of stars awaits us if we make it 'til quittin' thirty.

THE SACRIFICE

A chicken does not collapse immediately when its neck is wrung or its head is chopped off. Instead, the decapitated body runs around for several minutes without any apparent destination, except perhaps in search of its missing body part and away from its assassin. This was a particularly alarming scenario for a child to witness, and it seemed not to become less horrific with repeat performances. For this reason, I considered it a blessing that our family could afford to eat only one chicken per week, a staple of Sunday dinner.

In my youth, dinner was served at the noon hour and not at the end of day. The latter meal was supper, and often consisted of cornbread dunked into a glass of sweet milk and eaten with a large spoon, or an onion and slice of hog jowl placed between two pieces of cornbread. Unlike dinner during the week, when fried fatback or hog jowl was the only meat, Sunday dinners were special, and all stops were pulled out to prepare the best feast the family could afford.

Our family could not raise enough chickens to provide the one served each week for Sunday dinner. As luck would have it, Miz Eula Stewart, our across-the-road neighbor, raised a brood and sold her extras. Among my most dreaded errands was the frequent chicken purchase from Miz. Eula. In the rural Mississippi of my youth, buying a chicken did not involve a trip to a sanitary supermarket to select from birds already cleaned, cut into ready-to-cook parts, and nicely sealed in plastic wrap. The transaction involved following Miz Eula around her yard while she selected her mark and gave chase to the would-be victim, handily wielding a sharp hatchet in her right hand. It was difficult to say whether the hunt-to-kill process bothered Miz Eula, because like most folks in the poverty-ravaged Mississippi hill country, she had long since acquired the stoic demeanor that went with a lifetime of doing what-ever it took to get by and to keep food on the table. But I was yet tender, and the events that unfolded seemed unconscionable, except the next day when I was eating the headless casualty all battered in flour, salt, and pepper and deep fried. Still one had to respect the skill Miz Eula displayed as she overtook a Rhode Island Red. Once she had a chicken in her sights, the bird was as good as gone. With lightning speed, she would grab the squawking fowl by its neck and send it to the guillotine, either right there in midair or on the chopping block, which was also used by Mr. Stewart for splitting wood. At least the decapitation was quick, since she rarely missed, so a second blow was seldom required. I could have sworn I heard a collective sigh from the rest of the brood as they ceased their mad clucking, no doubt relieved that a fellow fowl had been sacrificed, allowing them to live yet another day.

This is where I became an accomplice. Once the de-capitated bird ceased its last run through the yard, Miz Eula would grab it by its legs, deposit it in a brown paper bag, and hand it to me in exchange for the fifty cents held in my free hand. Usually, there was enough movement in the bag to encourage me to run as fast as my legs would carry me back across the road to give the corpse to my mother. Mother would take the feathered kill into the backyard and drop it into a black iron cauldron full of boiling water. This was the same pot used for washing sheets, towels, and quilts on Mondays and Thursdays with water heated over a fire fed by kindling and split wood underneath, be-cause the wringer washing machine could accommodate only clothing and smaller items. Leaving the carcass in the hot water for a couple of moments loosened the feathers, making them easier to remove. Naked of its protective coating, the chicken looked less like a fowl and more like a dead person.

Mother would take the cadaver into the screened back porch, put it on the linoleum tablecloth that covered the worktable, and cut it into pieces for frying. Nothing was wasted, as she claimed the liver, gizzard, and heart to be prize parts of the chicken, though my siblings and I refused to eat a chicken's organs. Mother would no doubt have included the neck in this category had it not been attached to the severed head back in Miz Eula's compost pile. Once the pieces had been soaked in cold salty water overnight, Mother would fry up in a black iron skillet some of the best chicken known to mankind. I am not sure if it is a testament to my carnivorous nature or my hypocrisy, but as I sat eating the delicious meal, I completely forgot the horror show that led to the feast we shared. I felt no shame or remorse for the plight of the bird. I simply gnawed clean the bone of the one piece that was my allotment and looked forward to next Sunday's meal without a thought of the traumatic event that would unfold in order for me to savor it.

Mother always cut the chicken so that there was a pulley bone, as wish bones were called, for us kids to fight over. Once it had been stripped of meat, two of us would do battle over the tiny V-shaped bone and pull the ends in opposite directions until the bone broke into two pieces. The person with the largest portion of the bone in his hand at the conclusion of the pulling contest would be granted a wish. The results were inevitably contested, as the bearer of the shorter portion of the pulley bone contended a foul, no pun intended, had been committed. Whether this outcry negated the wish or whether it had already reached the big bird in the sky was not clear to me, but I chose to believe the wish had already taken wings.

I picture my mother eating the chicken's heart and liver, and then working to extract a few bites of meat from the one piece of chicken she unfailingly chose: the back. It somehow seems fitting that the woman who was the backbone of our family chose that piece of the chicken's anatomy. Still, occasionally we would ask her why she did not take a piece of chicken with more meat on it, and she always responded that the back was the best of the lot. Just as we accepted Mother's explanation that the two out-of-date dresses that hung in the chifforobe were still good enough to wear and clothes aplenty for her since she rarely went anywhere, we accepted her explanation of her strange taste in chicken. Such was our mother's way: to sacrifice for us even in the food she allowed herself to eat.

For many years now, Mother's closet has been bursting at the seams. She cannot wear all the clothes her children buy for her. Any specialty food item in which she expresses the slightest interest will be delivered by one of us on our next visit home. A trip is immediately planned to any destination she expresses an interest in seeing. At our family's Christmas dinner, Mother can hardly be detected behind the mound of presents she receives. Recently, at one of these gatherings, Cindy's son, Robert, and my son, Ryan, dubbed Mother the Don because her children and grandchildren treat her with much the same respect shown to Don Corleone in the *Godfather*. Seated beside Robert, she quietly says to him, "I want to visit with Dianne now," and Robert fetches Dianne. This ritual continues until Mother has visited individually with each child she does not see as frequently as those who live nearby.

My friends marvel that Mother's children are so attentive to her needs, and they sometimes ask me why that is. The way I see it, the reason is obvious. When one sacrifices for the good of the group, the survivors do not forget the gift that allowed them to live another day.

IT'S IN HIS KISS

S arah (pronounced Sayruh) arrived in our lives in the same way many good things land in a person's life. A tragedy brought her home to Randolph, a silver lining in that cloud. In addition to the other positive aspects she added to our lives, her change in residence increased Randolph's population by at least one percent. Sarah was by all accounts happily engaged in a career down in Columbus when her mother, Miz Eula, the noted chicken assassin, was felled by a stroke that permanently took away her ability to walk. One afternoon, Miz Eula collapsed on the ground in her front yard, and she never got up again. In those days, the damage from a stroke was rarely reversible, even if medical attention was administered promptly, which in Miz Eula's case it was not. In the blink of an eye, she was reduced from a strong, independent woman to a helpless invalid.

In keeping with the expectations of a good Southern daughter, as soon as Miz Eula was released from the hospital in Pontotoc, Sarah resigned from her job in Columbus and returned home to Randolph to care for her mother. Sarah arrived on a Sunday morning, in a gray fifties Ford

Thunderbird with a wheel affixed decoratively to the rear bumper. Watching from our front porch swing, Dena's and my attention could not have been more riveted had Sarah arrived in a pumpkin-turned-carriage. The Thunderbird was the finest automobile that had ever graced the black-top road that ran between the Stewarts' house and ours. The carriage did not belong to Sarah, we would soon learn, but in a way the driver did. We came to know the driver, Trapp, as Sarah's beau. Trapp was equally as handsome and elegant as his vehicle. From our vantage point across the road, he resembled a slightly grayer Cary Grant, and he dressed the part in his charcoal pleated slacks, white starched shirt, and light gray sports coat. His feet, clad in what had to be the only pair of white dress shoes ever worn by a man in Randolph, proved to us we were viewing a fine gentleman. After Trapp opened Sarah's car door, yet another touch of class, he glided across the yard with his sports coat slung casually over his left shoulder. I believe Dena and I fell in love before his foot hit the first step leading up to our neighbors' front porch.

Although our attention was focused primarily on Trapp, we did pay attention to Sarah as she made her debut in our lives. She was a rarity: a woman around thirty who Dena and I dubbed nice looking. Her thick, dark hair was pulled back from her face in a ponytail tied with a scarf that matched her blue dress. Her white full slip, visible beneath the nylon fabric of her dress, complimented the white patent leather sandals on her feet. Sarah's skin was darker than our mother's, and she was larger but by no means chubby. She and her driver made a striking couple: Mississippi's version of Cary Grant and Loretta Young. Their arrival created more intrigue for Dena and me than we had known in our short lifetimes.

Mr. Eugene Stewart hobbled down the front steps to welcome his daughter home to share his latest burden. His shoulders, already stooped, seemed more rounded than they had just a few weeks earlier. It was not as though he needed yet another heavy load to bear. His only son was the local oddity: a man who lived in a run-down house on Mr. Stewart's land, had no gainful employment, did not wear shoes, and was an encumbrance rather than an asset. Now, the helpmate on whom he had depended was incapacitated and his daughter was returning home permanently, a decision that, given the scarcity of available men in Randolph, carried with it an almost certain life sentence to spinsterhood. It was every father's desire to see his daughter happily married and producing his grand-children, so this was another disappointment for Eugene.

If Sarah shared any of these sentiments, she did not reflect them that Sunday or during the subsequent days that filled the ensuing years. She helped her dad and Trapp unload from Trapp's car all her clothes and other belongings and carry them up the steps into the house. The Stewarts' home was a well-kept, one story white house with six or seven wide steps leading to a front porch that ran the length of the house. Sarah's things were placed in the front room to the left of the central hallway, a room we had never been inside on our forays to the Stewarts' house to borrow a cup of sugar or to take Miz Eula some of the excess big boy tomatoes that grew in our garden. We did not see the room that day either, or ever for that matter. But it lives in my imagination as a majestic room filled with finery. For reasons that will unfold, that room I never saw became the one to which all others would be compared.

Trapp bid the family adieu around two o'clock in the afternoon, and Sarah escorted him to his car. With the car door ajar, he tipped Sarah's head back and gave her a light but lingering kiss that set my toes to tingling. A grown woman being kissed by a man in public during broad daylight was not the usual goings-on in Randolph, Mississippi, in the fifties, but it was a nice change from the perspective of the two spies across the road. It set us wondering what other titillating treats lay in store now that Sarah had arrived.

Sarah settled immediately into her new life. On Monday morning, she spread the bed quilts and blankets out on the shrubbery to catch the sun's rays. Freshly laundered curtains were soon hanging on the clothesline to dry. Such industry was not new to us, coming from a family who thought idle hands and minds were the devil's workshop and that cleanliness was next to godliness, but the apparent joy that accompanied her hard work was difficult to comprehend. You would have gathered from her demeanor that coming home was her idea, all part of her life's plan, and that household chores were reasons for joy. Dena and I were perplexed by this exotic creature who had alighted in our midst.

Over the coming months, more interesting patterns developed in the household across the road. The one of greatest import to Dena and me was that every three weeks, like clockwork, the gray Thunderbird pulled into the Stewarts' driveway between two and four o'clock on a Saturday afternoon. The man we called Trapp, although the name of every other man we knew was preceded by a title, emerged dressed in variations of his original attire and carrying with him a small valise such as Cary Grant might have used for travel. I mistakenly called it an overnight bag, but Dena set me straight. Since she was bookworm, and consequently, more sophisticated than me, she was acquainted with the proper names for accoutrements such as men's bags. Sarah always met Trapp on the front porch, where they would hug and exchange one kiss before going inside. We waited impatiently until around dusk for their return to our viewing area.

After supper, the handsome couple would retire to the porch, and we would become privy to the intimacy they shared. By that time, Mr. Eugene and Miz Eula were probably settled in for the night, allowing the love birds to direct their attention toward each other. The two would move to end of the porch closest to us but farther from Sarah's parents' room, holding hands, hugging occasionally, and periodically exchanging tender kisses. It would have taken a pair of large pliers to pry Dena and me away from the living room window where we were perched. Until Bobby and James graduated from high school and moved away, the living room also served as Dena's and my bedroom, and during the long days of summer, we were often in bed before the sun fully set. Our bedroom window was the orchestra section for the best theater Randolph had to offer.

As smitten as we were with the romantic rendezvous in our vicinity, we could watch for only so long before our seriousness gave way to laughter, as our giggle boxes got turned over for one reason or another. About that time, Mother would admonish us not to be so nosy and to get out of the window before she had to come in and remove us from it. Though her tone carried a threat, her words were wasted on us. The vignettes across the road were the most intriguing sights we had ever witnessed, and we would have suffered a tanning with a switch rather than miss them. In retrospect, this was our private soap opera, so unaware were we that we were living our own. Or perhaps, Sarah's was a more upbeat serial than the one unfolding in our house. Fortunately, the rating was PG, and just as the rating might have been adjusted, the beautiful pair would leave the porch and move the show inside, into the left front room where a soft light glowed. None of my real life liaisons have come close to the heights of romance I envisioned in that room I never saw, with its light blue velvet curtains, dark blue velvet bedspread, blue sculpted rug, and crystal chandeliers.

The Stewarts' lack of a telephone played well into Dena's and my insistence on being part of the lovers' tryst. Whenever Trapp wanted to talk to Sarah between his visits, he called our house and one of us would race across the road to summon her. Periodically, as a thank you, Trapp would bring us a bag of candy, further endearing him to us. His patterns were as predictable as rain following thunder, calling every Tuesday late in the day, arriving every fourth Saturday between two and four in the afternoon, and leaving the following day around eleven in the morning. Mother surmised that this pattern did not bode well for Sarah, but I did not understand the implication. Dena no doubt comprehended the meaning of Mother's remark since she knew *everything*.

The years wore on and nothing much changed in Sarah's life, until the summer the State Highway Department decided to build a new highway about two-tenths of a mile away from our house to bypass Randolph proper, replacing the portion of the highway that ran in front of our house. Children playing in the road were the only obstacles drivers faced on our stretch of the highway, since there was no traffic congestion or stop signs to impede their progress. For that matter, there was only occasional traffic on any part of Highway 9. Perhaps to appease the two merchants whose business might have been adversely affected by the rerouting, the State Highway Department resurfaced our rutted road with blacktop to fill the foot-deep potholes.

More than just a road changed that summer! Sarah had been in Randolph a few years when we received word about the new highway, which a half-century later we still refer to as the new road. Watching the construction crew operate their heavy equipment, which included bulldozers and paving machines, would have produced excitement enough for lifestyles as constant as ours, but Sarah once again expanded our horizons beyond our wildest expectations.

A few days after the crew reached our section of the highway, Sarah altered her daily schedule by adding an afternoon walk up to Mr. Onsby's store. About two o'clock, during the heat of the day, she would emerge through her front door dressed in a red nylon or red and white polka dot dress, both sleeveless with full, gathered skirts. Her pretty white sandals were on her feet, even though the road was all torn up and the broken concrete was sure to scuff her good shoes. Her dark wavy hair was tied back with a red nylon scarf that she'd designed from a remnant of the red nylon used to make the matching dress. Every afternoon, Sarah bounded up the hill in front of our house with such a sense of purpose and confidence you'd have thought it was something she'd done every day for years. She often returned sipping a cold, bottled, five-cent

Coca-Cola, happily quenching her thirst heightened by June's ninety-degree temperatures.

At about the same time that Sarah initiated her daily stroll to the store, the love detectives spotted the road workers' crew chief, a man we later came to know as Travis, taking a lot of interest in Sarah's daily walks. He seemed always to be parked on the side of the road at two o'clock, and when she approached, he would get out of his white truck to talk with her. His complexion was dark, probably from extended exposure to the Mississippi sun, and a he had strong, rugged appearance that made you think he would be a Marlboro smoker. Before we knew it, Travis had become a regular visitor for supper in the house across the road. After a few dates, Sarah escorted him to the front porch in the early evening to sit in the swing. At first, they just sat in the swing and talked. But it did not take many nights before they were not sitting but standing, and standing so close together you could hardly tell where one left off and the other one commenced. Their kisses did not have the gentleness we had detected when Trapp kissed Sarah. Sarah and Travis' kisses lasted so long that Dena and I started timing them to see how long the two participants could hold their breath. Unlike Trapp's gentle tip of her head, Travis held Sarah so tightly we worried he might hurt her, although I must admit to having been more thrilled by Travis' aggressive manner than worried for Sarah's safety. After a while they would go inside, and the soft light from the crystal reading lamp in the blue room would come on. From our vantage point, this concluded the feature film.

In spite of the drama he added to our lives, Travis was considered an unwelcome interloper by Dena and me. We hoped he would disappear when the construction on the road was finished. But after the roadwork was complete, his telephone calls to Sarah became more numerous— more frequent even than Trapp's. He sent us off to fetch Sarah a couple of times a week, with not one gift of candy to reward us for our trouble. That lapse in courtesy was not the only reason we preferred Trapp over Travis. Trapp was elegant and other-worldly, while Travis was rugged and commonplace.

For her part, Sarah seemed happier than ever! She juggled her two suitors quite expertly, blossoming in the process. Dena worried that Trapp would find out about Travis, and her concern that he was becoming suspicious was validated when Trapp altered his visitation pattern on one occasion. An unscheduled visit on a Wednesday afternoon almost upset the apple cart, but as luck would have it, Travis had not yet arrived, and when he drove by, he apparently spotted Trapp's car and continued down the road. That was when we realized that Travis knew about Trapp, leaving our beloved Trapp the uninformed member of the triangle.

A few weeks later, Trapp's car pulled into Sarah's driveway after Travis' mud-covered truck had arrived. Dena and I were breathless, anticipating a big scene. Would there be a fight to the finish for Sarah's love? Oh! How we hoped there would be. Would Trapp beat Travis to a pulp and send him, crushed and humiliated, down the road in his old white truck? Would Sarah plead with Trapp to forgive her indiscretions? And would he forgive her or reject her as Rhett Butler had Scarlett in *Gone with the Wind*? So many scenarios played out in our imaginations as Trapp knocked on the door and Sarah invited him inside. We waited with bated breath to see which man would stay and which one would leave.

In a short time, Trapp walked out of the front door and down the steps of the Stewarts' home. From where we were sitting, he looked pretty dejected. As he ambled from the house across the road to his car for the last time, Sarah did not run out of the house and fall on the ground, grab him by the pants legs, and plead with him not to go. She did not wedge herself between Trapp and the car door with laments like, "I can't go on living if you leave." To our chagrin, Sarah did not come out of the house at all. She stayed in the house with Travis. There was no heart-wrenching good-bye to provide closure for the fans across the road. Trapp just drove away, taking his gray Thunderbird with its decorative wheel, his Cary Grant looks, and all hopes of bags of candy and butterfly kisses out of our lives forever.

Travis' truck made regular appearances over the next few years, and for a while, Dena and I continued to live vicariously through the couple's front porch passionate embraces. Without Trapp's chic appearance and his car's stylishness, the saga soon lost its appeal for us. We wondered aloud from time to time what in heaven's name could have caused Sarah to choose the rough-cut, Levi-wearing Travis over the tailored and scrumptious Trapp. It was certainly not his appearance or the vehicle he drove. In our rating system, the way he hung around so much was a negative, while Trapp's flamboyant and less frequent arrivals were placed in the plus column. After all, our father came home once every three to four weeks, and we thought that was plenty of time for a man to be around. Although Sarah's penchant for Travis remained a mystery to us, we arrived at the only answer that made any sense to two young girls. Just one thing could have swung the scales in Travis' favor: His kiss.

SILENT SEPARATION

A black cat saved Larry's life. The feline that is purported to be a bad omen was the impetus for Uncle Lowell to take actions that saved our brother. Uncle Lowell and Aunt Lynda Merle had visited Mother and her seriously ill two-and-a-half-year-old son in Randolph and were headed back home to their home in Pontotoc when a black cat ran across the road directly in their car's path. Not a person typically given to superstitious tendencies, Uncle Lowell surprisingly took the cat's appearance as a sign and immediately turned the car around, put Mother and Larry in the backseat, and drove to the Pontotoc Hospital Emergency Room.

Larry's diagnosis was spinal meningitis, and his condition was critical. He lingered between life and death throughout the night. If Larry survived, the doctor advised Mother that he would be deaf, blind, or both. As our seven-month-pregnant mother stood watch over her baby boy, her water broke. Her pregnancy with Dena had been problematic from the start because she had contracted tuberculosis in the early months. When her doctor had ordered bed rest, Mother had come home from Mobile to stay with Mama and Papa, bringing her three boys with her and leaving Daddy behind in South Alabama, where he worked in the shipyards.

Larry survived, and so did Dena. The doctors said if Larry had not arrived at the hospital when he did, they could not have saved his life. Fortunately, his sight was spared, but his world became a silent one. Apparently, hearing does not cease immediately when the nerves responsible for transmitting sound waves to the brain are destroyed by Meningitis. Larry could hear for a short time after the damage occurred. Mother believes the sound diminished gradually, and that several weeks after his illness, he lost the last elements of his hearing. One day as she observed Larry at play in a sandbox, she noticed him gazing intently at the birds chirping overhead. He was transfixed by them, and as they flew away, he became uncharacteristically angry, screaming at the birds. Mother interpreted his behavior to mean that Larry's hearing ceased completely at that moment, and that Larry thought the birds had taken the sound with them as they disappeared into the distant sky.

Mother could not have anticipated the separation that would result from Larry's loss of hearing. As he entered a silent world, he became part of a society that operates differently than the one his hearing family negotiates, where sounds dictate so many of our behaviors. He entered a world absent the sounds of birds singing, music playing, water rushing, and the laughter and anger in the voices of those around him. On the other hand, he joined a world unencumbered by the distractions and demands of a verbal community. He claims it is a more peaceful world than we know and that he does not want to hear.

Larry's loss of hearing did not create a peaceful existence for Mother, the person responsible for his care. She relates stories of searching the woods around our house for him when, as a child, he failed to return home at the appointed hour. Time seemed less important to Larry than to the rest of us, and our fanaticism about measuring it appeared to perplex him. Even as a young adult, he once informed us he was going to visit a friend and would see us later, only to return three days later amazed to find us in a frenzy of worry. The friend, it turned out, lived in Alabama, and Larry had not meant to return on the day he left. He felt he had communicated this by the careful wording of his "see you later" farewell.

Mother's separation from Larry began in earnest when he reached school age. Like most states in the forties and fifties, Mississippi had only one school for the deaf, a state-run institution in Jackson, two hundred miles south of Randolph. When Larry turned six, Papa impressed upon Mother the reality that she already knew but could not face: it was imperative that her small son be sent away so that he could obtain an education equivalent to that provided for his hearing siblings. Mother was aware she had to eventually send Larry away to school, but she could not bear to send her six-year-old to a boarding school when the distance assured that he could return home only for summers and holidays. She delayed the decision for one year. The next August, she and Daddy drove to Jackson to deposit Larry in the institution that would become his home for nine months of the year for the next twelve years. It was one of the greatest losses our family had suffered.

If Larry's departure was hard for those of us left at home, it was devastating to him. How do you convey to a child of seven who does not read and has only a limited sign language with which to communicate that you are not abandoning him and that he will see you again? All Larry knew was that morning he had left his wonderful home in the woods where he roamed freely with his brothers, Bobby and James, and his sister, Dena (I was too young to join them but not too young to cry each time they left), and that afternoon he was abandoned by his parents to strangers in a sterile institutional environment. His heart was broken, and though he could not have known, Mother's was, too.

Larry's new environment, a large institution located in a city, was alien to him. The differences between this institutional facility and his country home were so great, at first he wasn't sure how to get his basic needs met. While outside at play in the schoolyard, he once peed behind a tree as he had done in the Mississippi countryside. When the teacher admonished him not to do that again, he was puzzled about where he was supposed to use the bathroom. As a result, he did not urinate or defecate for two days. By that time, he was in so much pain from the waste in his body that he could not sleep.

On the third day, when he was washing his hands, another boy came in and used one of the toilets, revealing to Larry the purpose of those shiny white fixtures. It surprised Larry that you could defecate in a nice, porcelain fixture and then flush away any evidence that it had been used for that purpose. He immediately appreciated the benefits of a modern bathroom, especially the shower that served the same purpose as the galvanized tub back home.

In time, Larry adapted to living away from home, and his deaf friends became his other family. Gifted intellectually, he was on the honor roll seven years in a row. He was even then showing glimpses of his gift as an artist, and friends and family flocked to him, badgering him to paint their portraits. After Larry adjusted to being away from his family of origin, his joyful nature returned.

Back home in Randolph, we counted the days in anticipation of Larry's summer visits and Christmas vacations, knowing he would bring with him the playful spirit that was uniquely Larry. Probably because he was away from us most of each year and because he was the only one with whom we didn't quarrel, Larry was the special sibling. He was equally elated to come home, hungry for the sight of his family and the familiar things he associated with his childhood. He reveled in our affection, especially Mother's, and he inhaled the dishes she prepared specifically because they were his favorites. But within a couple of months, Larry grew restless, lonely for the friends who shared his silent world. As the person who translated most family conversations for Larry, I probably unintentionally hastened his desire to return to his peers. It is surprising how many of the things people say reflect nothing more than idle chatter, just meaningless words to fill the void created by silence. As a result, I often tired of finger spelling and using the limited sign language I had mastered. Whenever that happened, I would tell Larry we were talking about the weather and wondering whether it was going to rain. He was understandably incensed by my response, having early on figured out my ploy.

As close as we were and as much as we loved each other, there was a divide between our worlds. Even though we talked with Larry through finger spelling and signs, he often resorted to written communication with us because we were too slow and inept in speaking with our hands compared to his deaf friends. Mother and Larry developed early in his life a communication technique that defies explanation. They actually *talk* to one another, she in a slightly louder voice than she would use with any of her other children and Larry in the broken English he learned before he lost his hearing. How they understand one another is a mystery! Even more perplexing is that when Mother calls Larry's name, although he may be facing another direction, he turns and looks at her. As children, we proved our hypothesis that it was only Mother who produced this phenomenon, since Larry was oblivious to his name being yelled at an ear-piercing decibel by a sibling.

Larry developed many talents in addition to his art-work, becoming proficient at a number of trades. His gifts are many, but the two he shares in common with his family are a large, loving heart and a smile that brightens the room. Larry is our family's reminder that while silence can separate people, love can transcend it.

THAT MEMPHIS WALK

When I am depressed or anxious, I walk. Not just for blocks but for miles. My favorite routes are those that are rote, requiring no decisions about direction. Southern society no longer values walking for any purpose other than exercise. In Birmingham, Alabama, when I walk to do my errands to the grocery store or cleaners, neighbors stop to offer rides. It seems odd to them that a person chooses to walk when she doesn't have to. I suspect my love of New York City is driven in no small measure by the fact that it is a city of walkers. Walking is in my blood, since in the not-so-distant past it was a necessity. For some of us, it still is.

Growing up, we walked because we did not have a car. We did, however, have a telephone. We proudly boasted our status as one of only two families in our neighborhood to possess one. We had a telephone because it was our father's only way to communicate with us when he lived and worked in Memphis. Just as we were in the minority when it came to folks with phones, we were the only folks within miles who did not own a car. Even Marlon, our across-the-road neighbor who was never gainfully employed during the fourteen years I knew him, had a shiny automobile sitting in his leaning, junk-filled garage.

We shared a party line with the McGregors, but since so few people had telephones, there was rarely a delay in placing or receiving a call. Most of the calls we received were long distance, from our father or Trapp. In those days, long distance calls were met with a sense of urgency. The person receiving the call yelled at the top of her voice to the designated recipient, *"It's long distance!"* The cost of long distance being what it was, we were trained to place person-to-person calls to be sure money was not wasted if the person we were calling was not home. If they were in, we called them back station-to-station. At that time, operators participated in all person-to-person calls, advising the person who answered the phone that only the designated party could accept the call. When one of her children traveled, Mother admonished us to signal our safe arrival by phoning person-to-person and asking for ourselves. Thanks, Ma Bell, for the peace of mind you afforded our mother at no charge.

Technically, we did own a car. It was simply housed one hundred miles north in Memphis with our father. Every three to four weeks, on a Friday night, he and the car graced us with their presence. In terms of which we were happier to see, the car won hands down. On Sunday afternoon before he returned to Memphis, Daddy would sometimes load us all into the sedan for a short ride. On one of these outings down the gravel road leading to the Oak Forest Cemetery, with five or six kids packed inside the car and me, the youngest at the time, sitting in Mother's lap, Daddy took a stab at teaching Mother to drive. She had more than a bit of difficulty getting a feel for it. After releasing a tirade of profanities, Daddy declared Mother a lost cause in the automotive department, and Mother readily agreed. To this day, I have nightmares about Mother driving the car in which I am riding, and in them I am aware she does not have control of the vehicle. A Jungian psychologist would have a field day with that subconscious manifestation.

Perhaps Mother came by her aversion to driving from her father. Like Mother, Papa had only one brief foray behind the wheel. In the twenties, he bought a Chevrolet, but after almost wrecking it on the way back home, decided the machine was not for him. The Chevy was embraced by his son Lowell, age twelve, for the short time it remained in the household. By Mama's account, when Papa was away, Lowell drove her and her daughters wherever they wanted to go.

I remember Uncle Lowell as a great driver, speeding from point to point in his push-button Chrysler with not one wreck, or so he said. In his eighties, after he lost most of his vision, he drove an old blue truck. By that time, he was forever running into light poles, but he never did hit a person. I suppose colliding with poles did not qualify as an accident in his definition of auto mishaps. His good work as one of Pontotoc's few druggists and as a member of the First National Bank Board of Directors must have earned him special dispensation from the law enforcement community in his later years. In his day, he was known for getting up at all hours of the night to meet a parent at the drugstore to provide medicine for a sick child. I guess some of the local folks never forgot his kindness. When he was pushing eighty-five, he drove his old blue truck down to the Mississippi Highway Patrol Driver's License Office to renew his license and asked for Jack, one of the officials who felt kindly toward him. The fellow he spoke to was quite taken aback and advised Uncle Lowell that he *was* Jack. Always quick on his feet, Uncle Lowell responded that he had not recognized Jack out of uniform, to which Jack allowed that he was wearing his uniform. He renewed Uncle Lowell's license and told him to get the hell out of there and go straight home. When recounting this story,

Uncle Lowell laughingly alleged that he hit a light pole when he was leaving the parking lot that day.

Colliding with light poles was not a problem for Aunt Louella, Mother's sister, but she did run over Mother a few years back. While waiting for Aunt Louella to pick her up for a shopping expedition, Mother sat down under the carport to visit with Uncle Lowell. Resting on folding chairs worn from years of use, the two of them were admiring Mother's flower garden which was particularly colorful that June thanks to an abundance of May showers and Miracle-Gro. As Aunt Louella rolled up the drive and into the carport, she became distracted by something on the dashboard and paid no attention to the forward movement of the vehicle. Observing that she was not stopping, Mother and Uncle Lowell sought to get out of her way. Uncle Lowell was able to push his chair back far enough to avoid major injury, though he did say Aunt Louella ran over his foot as she rolled past. Mother was either not so agile or not so lucky. She stood up and started backing away from the oncoming vehicle and, having backed up to the point that she could go no farther, was overtaken by the runaway automobile. The next thing she knew, she was under the vehicle with only her head protruding below the front bumper. By then, a loud argument was raging between

Uncle Lowell and Aunt Louella. He was threatening to tell Louella's son, Phillip, to take her car keys away from her, and she was vehemently objecting. Mother was able to grab hold of the car's grill and pull herself out from under the car, while Uncle Lowell shifted his lament to the need to file a claim on Mother's homeowner's policy to cover the cost of the broken lawn chairs. It was irrelevant to him that the chairs cost less than twenty dollars when they were new and that the deductible on Mother's homeowner's policy was two hundred and fifty dollars. Ironically, *he* was intent upon chastising *Aunt Louella* for driving carelessly. Neither he nor Aunt Louella considered taking Mother to the emergency room to assess the damage to her person. Instead, Mother dusted herself off and went inside to regroup, change her clothing, and comb her hair. A few minutes later, she emerged from the house neatly coiffed, climbed into the car with Aunt Louella, and they headed off as planned to a shoe store in Tupelo.

Mother did not mention this incident to any of her children. However, a few days later, she became dizzy and fell off the front porch. She was banged up pretty badly, and this time she was treated in the emergency room. She was still experiencing dizziness when I arrived several days later, so we made a return trip to the ER. The attending physician asked if Mother had sustained the knot on the back of her head as well as the one on her forehead in the fall from the porch. She replied matter-of-factly, "No, I got that one on the back of my head when my sister ran over me." I am not sure who was more stunned, the doctor or me, as Mother recounted the tale of how Aunt Louella had run her over.

Perhaps the most notable driver of our youth was Bobby, who soon after going to work in Memphis was the proud owner of the fastest Plymouth ever to leap over the hill leading to our house. His car was noted for never taking that hill on all four tires. After he bought the car, he was perpetually en route from one place to another at break-neck speed. So renowned was he for his alarming speed that once when I was in Mr. Dolan's general store, a local woman rushed her two children off the road and into the store, exclaiming, "Get out of the road; here comes that wild Bobby Flaherty." I crouched behind the canned goods counter, not wishing to be recognized as one of Bobby's sisters on that particular occasion.

Even though Mother and her children did, for the most part, walk to places to which others rode, there were two notable exceptions. We rode to the cotton patch to chop or pick cotton, transported by Uncle Howard, Mr. Lerone

Bray, or Mr. Lamar Lindsey, and we rode with the mailman on the rare occasion when we had to go to "town," as we referred to Pontotoc, the county seat. On those occasions, we flagged down Mr. Talent, the mail carrier who ran the route from Pontotoc to Sarepta. The exciting part of this ride was that the passenger was in charge of placing the incoming mail into the boxes on the side of the road opposite the driver's seat, removing outgoing mail from the boxes when the red flag was standing upright, and returning the red flag to the inactive position. Dena and I usually took these rides to town together, so we alternated the role of assistant mailman, arguing the whole trip about whose turn it was.

Mama and Papa introduced us to the U.S. Mail Service as a form of transportation. They lived two miles southwest of us down Highway 9, and at least twice a week walked to our house on some errand. Sometimes it was to bring fresh milk along with a saucer of butter Mama had beaten in the churn that same morning from the cream that had risen to the top of the milk. She fashioned the butter in a circle and used a fork to make designs around it. Every Monday, Mama and Papa came to help Mother build a fire under the iron pot in our backyard and wash jeans, quilts, sheets, and blankets, and help her hang those heavy loads on the clotheslines tied between the cedar and oak trees in our side yard, where they would freeze before drying on cold winter days. Mama walked to our house to help Mother quilt the coverlets that were stacked four and five deep on our beds to keep us warm on cold winter nights. She showed up more frequently in the summertime to help with canning and sometimes to bring some clothes she had fashioned—cutting her own patterns from old newspapers—and sewn for us to wear to summer school. In the summertime, Papa hitched rides with Mr. Talent so that he could bring the lawn mower to cut our grass. Early the following morning, he walked back to our house and rode home in the mail truck with the mower planted firmly in the back.

Although Mama and Papa made an equal number of forays to our house, it was Mama's visits I cherished. The straw hat that covered her closely cropped and tightly permed white hair was the first thing we saw when she appeared on the horizon. No matter how hot the weather, you could count on Mama to be wearing a large-brimmed hat, long-sleeved dress, and cotton hose held above the knee by garters so tight they left an indention in her skin when they were removed "ova" evening, as she called dusk. It was a source of dismay to her that her granddaughters exposed their bodies to the sun's rays, causing browned skin that she equated with white trash. In retrospect, we should have taken Mama's advice on skin care, because at one hundred and one, when her body and mind gave out, her skin was flawless, devoid of age spots. Unfortunately, she was correct when she lamented that she was wasting her breath on us, just like "fartin' in a whirlwind."

Aside from the hat, Mama's movements distinguished her from other passers-by. Hers was a quick, hurried gait, with a purpose that bespoke the many important things she needed to accomplish before sundown. Mama was not intimidated by traveling alone along the unpopulated stretch of highway that gave me the willies. Standing five foot two inches tall and weighing one hundred and ten pounds soaking wet, there was no mistaking that she was a force with which to be reckoned. She was the first woman I knew who shook hands with men when introduced, and they seemed to respect her as much as they did Papa. Maybe they also appreciated the light and life she brought with her wherever she went. Her vitality energized the people and things she touched. I wanted to follow her every step so that I could hear about what she had seen and heard on the way to our house. She noticed which plants were blooming and who was getting ready to plant their crops, and she learned about our neighbors' lives. Folks came out to greet her when they saw her walk by, so she acquired all sorts of interesting information. She turned down offers of rides, insisting she needed the exercise.

I doubt that Papa was wearied from the trip, either, so enthralled was he in the spirit of God. Either that or he was dissociating, and I have never been sure which it was. Regardless, Papa was in this world but not of it. Though he moved among us doing the things that were needed, he traveled above us. If you walked with Mama, she spun yarns about the neighbors or things that happened years ago. If you accompanied Papa, he shared gospel stories, especially parables, or taught you a Bible verse. Sometimes he rhythmically repeated under his breath one of the Native American chants taught to him by his mother. Mama was the eyes and ears of all things real, and Papa was the dreamer of things that cannot be seen.

Mama's insistence on walking served her well in her later years. At ninety-seven, a broken hip might have permanently curtailed a less fit person's movement, but not Lula Mae's. It is, by the way, a testament to her sense of balance that she did not incur a fracture while climbing up the ladder to check on things on top of the house, as she was wont to do. All through her nineties, she and

Uncle Lowell, who lived two doors down from her by then, entertained themselves by arguing about Mama's ladder. Each time he caught her on it, he took it around back of the house and put it in the shed. Not to be pushed around by her own son, Mama waited for him to leave home so she could sneak the ladder out of the shed and drag it around the house to handle some perceived defect she could not otherwise reach. She made it a point to return the ladder to the shed before Uncle Lowell came home. In the name of protecting Mama from herself, some well-meaning neighbor would tell Uncle Lowell they had seen her up on the rooftop again, and he would go into a tirade with Mama. Then the back and forth started all over again.

In the end, Mama's hip gave way of its own accord one night. Because she was otherwise in fine physical condition, the doctors decided her quality of life was good enough and her heart adequately strong to merit a hip replacement in spite of her advanced age. Mama proved to be a good patient until she was sent to a rehab facility to convalesce. She refused to adapt to that environment. When asked about the source of her discontentment, she advised us she had to get out of that place because there was nobody there but old people. "Old" was not a term Mama would ever have used to describe herself. She came home two weeks later, aided by a walker that she disdain-fully threw out the side door of the house.

On Mother's Day, three months after her fracture, I trav-eled to Mississippi to take Mother and Mama out to lunch in Tupelo. "Oh the fire!" (pronounced far) she proclaimed, a phrase she used when she flatly dismissed any subject. She told me she would be seen in public when she would not embarrass herself by using a walker. Sure enough, in August of that year, she strode unassisted into her ninety-eighth birthday celebration, decked out in her Sunday best with a brooch pinned to her lapel, signifying she was fully presentable for a public appearance.

The women we knew wore flat-soled shoes except on Sundays when some of them wore dress shoes with one-inch heels to church services. Mother still owned a couple of pairs of high heels from her years in Memphis, and Dena and I tramped around in them each time we could sneak them out of the chifforobe. When Dena and I, in turn, graduated from eighth grade, we pleaded to shave our legs and wear two-inch heels to our graduation exercise. Mother agreed with one proviso: we must first learn how to walk like ladies, which she said meant we could not ap-pear to be stepping over cotton rows. This was no small challenge, since we had considerably more experience maneuvering between cotton plants than walking in high heels. We must have managed not to look like we were kicking clods of dirt, because each of our eighth grade photos shows white heels at the base of our skinny legs.

Sunday afternoons, after our traditional lunch of fried chicken and creamed potatoes was devoured and the dishes washed, dried, and put away, we all retired to the front porch to sit in rockers, the swing, and straight-backed chairs tipped back against the side of the house. Before we reached dating age at fifteen, about the only thing to do on those afternoons was to count out-of-state car tags, a contest that lost steam pretty quickly when only two or three foreign tags were spotted on a good day. Invariably, around three o'clock, my siblings and I, joined by neighbors Belinda and Randy, took a walk through the center of Randolph and back home via the new road. As we walked, we held hands and shared our dreams of future days, particularly the fun we would have on Sunday afternoons when we could ride in cars. We talked about boys, clothes and the cars we would drive someday, cars that would take us to a bigger and more exciting world beyond our blacktop road. We were sometimes pursued by unknown people in their cars, but whether they were well-meaning folks wondering why seven children were wandering the roads or perverts seeking victims, we never knew, since we ran like the wind and scattered in all directions until the perceived threat was gone.

As was common in those days, Mother permitted her kids a tremendous amount of freedom. The world was open to us as long as the destination was within walking distance and as long as we reported for dinner at eleven and supper at five, and returned for our baths before dark. When James, Bobby, and Larry were six to twelve, they rode their bicycles miles away, climbing weather towers and warring with their BB guns and sling shots, miraculously reaching adulthood with their eyes, arms, and legs intact and not having been prosecuted for shooting anyone. By the time Dena and those of us younger than her were ready to ride, our family could no longer afford a bicycle. Consequently, we walked everywhere. We walked with some frequency to swim in Fulton's Pond, a pool of water covered with algae and infested with water moccasins. This was the same body of water where I was baptized, buried with Jesus and the water moccasins, washed clean of my sins by the muddy water.

Papa and Mama's visits became more frequent after Daddy walked out on us for good. That was also when

Mother began her nightly vigil, pacing up and down the front yard. After she put us to bed, Mother walked and cried, seeping desperation and voicing her feelings of hopelessness, asking God why, and praying for an end to her dreaded existence. With equal fervor, we beseeched God not to let her die. It was not just that she was our only *remaining* parent, but that for all practical purposes, she was the only one we had *ever had*. Eventually, Mother stopped walking the yard at night. She also stopped walking to Mr. Onsby's store, or to the school just up the hill to attend our events, or to church with us on Sunday morning, though she still hustled us out the door for all those occasions. Mother did not leave our yard for several years, except to go to the cotton fields or to Mama and Papa's at Christmas, harp singing day on the third Sunday in June, or the Fourth of July. She no longer sang as she worked in the house, cooking our food, cleaning our home, and ironing our clothes. A blank stare replaced the look of serenity we had seen on our Mother's face before hope walked out of her eyes.

The one thing about Mother that did not change AD (after Daddy) was the way she walked, albeit limited to our yard. Mother was a looker—five foot seven and slender, with legs like a long drink of water, as they said in those days—and her walk was a head turner. Dena and I were mortified by our mother's style of walking, so different was it from the strides of most of the people we knew. We labeled it her "Memphis Walk," assuming she had acquired that head held high in the air, straight back, perfected sway of the hips on her brief stint in Memphis where she, Daddy, and the first three boys had resided in better days. Mother's stride reflected a sophistication that separated her from us, and for that reason, it presented a threat to us. I now recognize it as a proud walk of someone who refused to lose any measure of elegance she had garnered just because our father had planted her penniless and without transportation back home in Mississippi's red dirt countryside. As an adult, I have seen that walk in beautiful women, a walk that says, "You can look all you want, but I am way beyond your reach." It agitated Dena and me no end to see our mother flaunt her city ways. Consequently, we made all manner of fun—behind her back, of course, lest she send us walking out back to select our own switch.

At eighty-nine, Mother's body is breaking down, though thankfully, not her mind. Mentally, she is more with us than she was in our youth. She has not lost any of her determination to keep going when things are tough, or that proud manner that makes her seem regal. Recently, as we watched her struggle to stand and walk, Dena whispered to me, "What I wouldn't give to see that Memphis Walk just one more time."

SUMMERTIME AND THE LIVIN' AIN'T EASY

Our forefathers were farmers, among their other professions, and we continued that tradition. Our farm was too far north of the Delta to produce bounty crops and too small to provide more than sustenance for our family. Actually, it consisted of a house, a barn, and few acres of land purchased for two thousand dollars with a portion of the ten thousand dollars our father received as a legal settlement after a drunk driver jumped a curb and ran over him on a Memphis sidewalk, virtually destroying his right leg. I was four when that misfortune occurred. Dena and I awoke one morning to find Mama in our kitchen, cooking breakfast on the black wood stove. While we slept, Mother had been ferreted away to Memphis to be with our father.

When Mother and Daddy returned home, it was difficult to say which of the two was more severely wounded. His leg had been mangled in the accident and would never fully regain its previous function. Judging from Mother's countenance, something inside her had also been shattered. Through our clandestine operations—eavesdropping on a conversation between Mother and Mama—Dena and I pieced together the reason for the latter injury. In the hours after the surgery, while our father was incapacitated, Mother had been asked to provide hospital administration information that required her to look in our father's wallet. Folded inside his wallet was a small piece of paper that altered her perception of their marriage: a receipt in the amount of forty-five dollars for a woman's Helbros watch. Our father did not give our mother such luxurious presents, and since that fine time-piece did not grace her arm, the record of its purchase told a story Mother did not want to read. Within hours, a heavy piece of machinery crushed our father's leg, and a thin piece of paper crushed our mother's heart. Yet, she brought our father home to convalesce, and she cared for him until he could return to work. Then we all moved into the rundown house he purchased for our family.

The house and farm in Randolph was the first residence our family had owned and would be my home until I left at age seventeen to seek employment in Memphis. Although it was only a mile from the small house we rented behind Obie Grubbs, the same man our father cut off from the hearse transporting his father-in-law to his gravesite, I resented the move. My best friend was Mr. Grubbs' son, Keith, and he shared his tricycle with me, as well as the sugar and biscuits his mother, Miz Fadrel, made for him every morning. I was allowed to roam freely with Keith, and even though I had more freedom than most four-year-olds, it did not extend as far away as Keith's house after our move one mile up the road.

Our new home consisted of four rooms built around a central fireplace, with a hearth and mantle in every room. In keeping with the progress of the fifties, the hearths had been sealed off with clapboard to make way for butane gas heaters. The house was semi-circled by a porch, home to a swing and several straight-backed chairs occupied by family members and a neighbor or two on weekday evenings and after the Sunday midday meal during the spring, summer, and fall. In the South of my youth, the larger the family, the more guests it attracted, and since ours was the largest family in the community, we generally had at least one extra person seated at our supper table. That seems particularly ironic given our distinction as one of the poorer families in our neck of the woods. Whatever we lacked in funds, our mother more than surpassed in family pride, so to my knowledge, she never told any outsider we had no food for them. Family meals, unlike family business, were to be shared with outsiders.

In rural Mississippi communities of that era, the central conversational topic of spring, summer, and fall was that year's crop. The major money crop was cotton, but the vegetables produced on small farms were essential for putting food on the table for the entire year. The farming process began with burning off the fields to prepare the ground for plowing and planting. Our mother was in charge of burning the remnants of the prior year's garden and the adjoining grass, a task she savored. Conventional wisdom held that you chose a day with calm winds to burn patches of ground so as to avoid an unmanageable spread of fire. For some reason, our mother favored blustery weather for this chore. Our brother, James recalls the foreboding sense that came over him when, on windy March days, he gazed out the schoolhouse windows and spotted the sway of trees, imagining our mother lighting the match to the underbrush behind our house that would produce a raging inferno. To her credit, only once was the volunteer fire department summoned to extinguish the blaze after the fire had leapt onto the Tutors' property and threatened their home place.

Farming on our land was limited to a vegetable garden and two truck patches. The official designation as a truck patch applies to plots near the road where produce is sold to passers-by or to merchants. In our vernacular, a truck patch differed from a garden in size, dimensions, and the kind of crops it contained. A garden was usually wider than a truck patch and enclosed with fencing to protect the tomatoes, peas, beans, cabbage, and other tempting fare from rabbits and other marauders. Truck patches were not fenced and were reserved for less tantalizing crops like corn and Irish or sweet potatoes. Gardens required a great deal more tending than these plots, with care exercised to remove the grass without harming the plants, softening the soil around the plants to hasten their growth. Truck patch rows received their share of hoeing, but once the corn was side-dressed a time or two and had grown to a height where the ears had begun to tassel, keeping them clean of weeds was less important. Side-dressing sounds more exotic than it is, not akin to cross-dressing but instead a shallow tunnel beside the corn that is filled with fertilizer to speed the plants' growth. The preferable fertilizer was not store-bought, but manure, the same stimulant used by modern-day organic farmers whose produce commands premium prices.

After Papa coaxed Old Dan to pull the plow through the furrows, uprooting the grass, my siblings and I were charged with keeping the garden free of weeds. One June day as we hoed the garden for the umpteenth time, my younger sister, Betty Jo, proclaimed us to be the best hoers in the county. At the tender age of seven or eight, she said this with sincere pride, but being a more sophisticated twelve or thirteen, I admonished her not to repeat this observation to another soul.

When the peas and beans were "filled out," Mother picked the vines clean and deposited the harvest into pails. Those buckets full of beans and peas were dumped into a galvanized tub on the side porch for shelling. This was the same tub in which we all bathed in the backyard each night during the spring, summer, and fall seasons and once a week in front of the kitchen's butane heater during the coldest winter weeks. Preparing the harvest for canning was the kids' domain. The Mississippi temperatures had generally reached one hundred degrees Fahrenheit in the shade by the time of year this chore commenced, and when you put a bunch of rowdy kids to work in that environment, more than beans can snap. By the time we had spent a few days getting the vegetables ready for Mother to can, she was ready to can us. Fingers dyed purple from shelling purple hull peas, and butts numbed from sitting on wooden slats from dawn to dusk were not as sore as our attitudes toward each other by the time the job was complete. Too much togetherness gave birth to many a quarrel among the shellers and snappers. You can sit in a straight chair, mindlessly ripping peas from a pod, for just so long before the monotony turns to disgust with your co-workers, and the superficial chatter of pre-and-post-pubescent girls and their brothers turns nasty.

It was during one of our heated exchanges that I dodged a well-deserved left from Dena and fell off the porch, impaling myself on a stob. The stob just missed a jugular, which was appropriate since I had aimed for hers with the offending remark. A stob is the remains of a bush that has been cut back nearly to the ground. A stob might be called a trunk if it was the remains of a tree, or it might be called a stake by some. But we referred to it a stob, and having been almost fatally stabbed by one, I consider the designation to be quite accurate.

Mother didn't allow us to participate in the actual canning process. That's because the process required a pressure cooker, and she was convinced it would one day blow the roof off the kitchen and take one of our heads with it. Her concern was not unfounded, since the pressure had forced the lid off a previous cooker. A greasy spot on the ceiling reminded us of a stewing hen that had once been catapulted upward by the powerful steam escaping from a poorly supervised container—another reminder that "keeping a lid on it" may not always be possible.

Preserving food by canning was crucial since the summer's bounty fed us through the winter, and freezers weren't readily available. My favorite preservation process was the one employed in making sauerkraut. This was principally because Mother and her mother, Mama, stayed outside with us kids to kraut rather than working inside canning, since the cabbage could not be put into jars until it had fermented for a week or ten days. In our family's vocabulary, kraut is both a noun and a verb. Krauting is the activity engaged in to produce the kraut.

When it was time to kraut, Mother, Mama, and us kids found a comfortable place under a shade tree, to avoid getting the cabbage all over the porch. A five-gallon earthen churn was placed in the middle of the chopping circle. Each of us held a dishpan and a knife in our laps, and as we chopped wedges of cabbage into tiny pieces, Mama regaled us with stories of the haunted house down on the Spikes Road where she and Papa had once lived. Apparently, the house was haunted by poltergeists that derived their kicks in non-damaging but annoying ways. According to Mama's account, each time the family left the house, the spirits moved the furnishings from the inside of the house to the outside, depositing the pieces on the front porch. Upon the family's return, they had to carry the furniture back inside. When we inquired how Mama knew it was not just a local prankster who relocated the furniture, she related an episode in which some of the local men had kept watch, hiding in the woods to catch the culprits. They reportedly saw no one come or go, and yet the household trappings were rearranged. Mama also told us that on the night her own mother died, glancing outside the window of that same house, she had seen two men dressed in white carrying a casket. Her mother took her last breath within the hour.

These were some of our earliest encounters with the supernatural, and vicarious though they were, they undoubtedly influenced our perceptions of reality. Our mother, a quiet, reserved woman who never told us stories, listened respectfully while Mama spun these yarns. Mama's character, as solid as the Rock of Gibraltar, was not one to which fits of fancy could be attributed. Consequently, her stories carried unquestioned credence in our young minds. If Mother disbelieved them, she never said so.

Another reason for my love of krauting involves a sense other than the sixth one. Kraut contains lots of salt and a bit of sugar added during the chopping process, and we were free to nibble on this savory delight to our hearts' content. Little is more pleasing to an Irish girl's palate than a salty treat. That one rivaled the more expensive and infrequent one obtained at Larry Onsby's store: a five cent bottled Pepsi Cola with a bag of Planters salted peanuts dumped inside it. The only better treat was one of Papa's Lingreen watermelons that he painstakingly tended to ensure the cool space underneath Mother's bed was filled during July and August. Mid-afternoons, the family gathered on the grass in the side yard, bringing a large melon, a shaker of salt, a large butcher knife, and a bundle of spoons.

Speaking of stores, our principal one rolled. We raised our vegetables and purchased an occasional piece of fatback or hog jowl from Mr. Onsby's or Mr. Dolan's local general store, but the staples were purchased from Mr. Carter, a peddler who drove through every Monday in a truck referred to as a rolling store. Through my young eyes, our peddler looked exactly like the man on the Lipton Tea box, and for years, I thought they were one and the same. I also thought the man in the moon had an uncanny resemblance to them both, which added intrigue to the purveyor of the rolling store. The back of his truck was set up to house the small store, and since he carried most essentials needed by country folks, we relied on his weekly trips. If we were home, we would "meet the peddler," a phrase that meant we met him at the door of his store and waited while he filled our order. Sometimes, he let us kids climb up into the truck bed and watch him gather the items. On autumn days when we were in the fields picking cotton, Mother left her list, along with a ten dollar bill, under a rock on the front porch, and Mr. Carter would place the groceries and her change by the door. Mother habitually put three packs of Wrigley's chewing gum on the list—Juicy Fruit, Spearmint, and Doublemint—and to this day, you won't catch her without a pack of Wrigley's gum in her purse.

Cotton and vegetables weren't the only things we picked. We harvested every blackberry within a two-mile radius of our house. Blackberries grow wild exclusively in areas heavily infested with snakes and red bugs, or chiggers as some called them. During late June and early July, some combination of Dena, BJ, Cindy, Tony, the neighbor's children, Belinda and Randy, and me frequently took one-gallon pails over the hill and through the barbed-wire fence into Mr. Jay's pasture in search of blackberries. We never sought permission to traverse his land to gather berries or for the myriad other adventures that required us to trespass through his property. The presence of a fence might have deterred the less adventurous, but we knew the fences were for keeping cows in, not people out.

Besides, this one consisted of just three strands of barbed wire, not the more serious electric wire from which you could not escape if you were unlucky enough to grab one, as each of us did once and only once in our childhood. We walked about a mile past his fishing pond to get to the spot where the berries flourished. On other outings, including chopping cotton or hoeing the garden, we kept as much of our skin exposed as possible to stay cool, but when on berry-picking expeditions, we covered ourselves from head to toe. Blackberry bushes house millions of tiny thorns, and to get to the best berries, you have to go through the middle of those clusters.

Snakes were another threat to the scavengers of wild fare. One day, after a particularly successful foray, Dena spotted a cottonmouth. Screaming at the top of her lungs for the rest of us to look out for the viper, she started running away. Not realizing the snake was between the two of us, I followed her lead. I tossed my pail straight up into the air, spilling the day's harvest, and according to Dena, jumping directly over the coiled reptile. She was so disconcerted by my close encounter with the snake that she threw her pail down in order to run unencumbered. The others followed suit. Once we were several hundred feet away from danger, we calmed down sufficiently to realize we could not return home devoid our pails. We somehow managed to summon the courage required to retrieve our buckets before we made a beeline for home. Mother just shook her head when we presented our empty pails, apparently not so much shaken by our close encounter with death as the knowledge that a blackberry cobbler would not grace the supper table that night. The smell of cobbler was replaced with that of kerosene to kill the only thing that we brought home that day: an abundance of red bugs embedded in the folds of our skin.

Our alarm upon encountering the cottonmouth seems odd in light of our how routinely we interacted with other varieties of vipers. On days when we were not otherwise engaged in hoeing, pea shelling, or berry picking, we hung out at Indian Creek, a small tributary adjacent to our property. The shallow creek covered with huge rocks had been home to the Choctaw Indian tribe of North Mississippi. It was populated with vast numbers of arrowheads that we retrieved and immediately lost, and with copperheads and moccasins that terrorized us and us them in turn. We claimed the rocks as our homes, removing the occasional vagrant from his sunny perch on our faux front porch by tossing rocks from the embankment. We took these contacts in stride, just as we took it in stride that on days when we swam at Fulton's pond, we had to jump out of the water occasionally to let a moccasin swim to its destination. Each time we left the house, Mother cautioned us to stay away from snakes much as parents today caution their children to avoid strangers. How she envisioned we could do that is beyond me, but I must credit her with having what appears to be a strong prayer frequency with God. Not a single one of us suffered a bite during our youth. At age forty, I was bitten in the garage of my suburban home in Birmingham, Alabama, by a displaced copperhead finding a cool reprieve from the summer's heat on the cement floor. No doubt, that snake sent up a victorious spray of venom to the serpent spirit in the sky, proclaiming, "We finally got one of Nellie's younguns!"

Our summer activities included at least one creative enterprise. One year, we spent most of the summer building a boat from scrap lumber we pulled off our barn and wood we found throughout the countryside. We sawed and nailed until we had completed a sad-looking craft. We failed to grasp the importance of caulking the small spaces between the planks. Our vessel complete, we hoisted it onto our shoulders and, straining under the weight, hauled it across Mr. Jay's property to the place designated for our maiden voyage. The selected body of water was smaller and shallower, if somewhat more snake-ridden, than Mr. Jay's fishing pond. Each of us wanted to be the captain of the first cruise across the pond, but fortunately, someone in the group had the foresight to suggest we send the craft across the water without the crew just to make sure it floated. Our summer's work sank to the bottom of the pond in a matter of minutes.

Our most successful endeavor was making flip-flops from cardboard and yarn after our cousin Hilda modeled the real ones for us. At ninety-nine cents a pair, the actual shoes were out of our reach. Still too young to hire out to chop cotton, we had no other opportunities to earn that much money. It is certainly true that necessity is the mother of invention. Our cardboard rip-offs didn't make that cool popping sound when we walked, but they gave the visual impression we sought. More important, our exercise seemed to tap into the cosmic realm, as Aunt Lynda Merle showed up at our house just days later with pairs of real flip-flops for all Mother's girls and for Tony. We spent the next few days competing to see who could make their shoes pop the loudest.

Once you were old enough, chopping cotton was summer's money-making venture, though it lasted only a few weeks. The nature of the work allowed the choppers to wear shorts and sleeveless shirts, thereby ensuring an enviable tan. Walking up and down rows of cotton only a foot tall, taking out all but three or four stalks on each mound and any grass that remained after plowing was a piece of cake compared to the arduous autumn job of picking cotton. In addition, Mother and Dena didn't usually chop cotton with me, so I was free to express my more bohemian nature. I was surrounded by a group of less refined, high-spirited types who told off-color jokes, smoked cigarettes, chewed tobacco, and were in fact the type of hooligans whose company I craved. They had many skills to teach, including how to spit tobacco juice out the side of your mouth and use your mouth to make rings when exhaling smoke.

The routine summer fare was rarely but happily interrupted by an opportunity to spend a week in Pontotoc. Uncle Lowell and Aunt Lynda Merle, who had no children of their own, sometimes invited Dena and me to their house for Hospitality Week, a Pontotoc tradition. The local citizenry stopped every car sporting an out-of-state tag and treated them to lemonade and cookies. Fortuitously, the welcome stand was set up on Oxford Street directly in front of Uncle Lowell's house. Just before one o'clock in the afternoon, Dena and I perched ourselves on lawn chairs in his front yard and watched in wonder until five p.m. the spectacle of Pontotoc's hospitality. This pleasure surpassed even that of the early mornings, when Aunt Lynda Merle allowed us to spend an hour in the attic playing house and walking her magical doll around as though it was our child. This was the same doll Uncle Lowell had given to Aunt Lynda Merle one year on their anniversary, with a large diamond ring attached to its wrist. Aunt Lynda put a stop to our morning adventures after I refused to come down at the appointed time one day and broke a lamp as I dodged her. Poor Dena lost upstairs privileges along with me. At night, while Aunt Lynda Merle and Uncle Lowell finished their bowls of orange sherbet, Dena and I chased lightning bugs in the back yard and wondered why their lights went out once they were lodged into Mason jars covered by punctured lids.

The summer getaways that topped Hospitality Week were those to Memphis and Clarksdale. A couple of times, out of the blue, our brother James and his wife, Marie, or our sister Ann and her husband, Harvey, came to get us to spend a week in their homes. Memphis's nighttime skyline was spectacular, and watching airplanes take off and land at the Memphis airport kept us spellbound for hours. It was on one of those forays that Larry and I were introduced to pizza, which we both tasted with trepidation and to which we were immediately addicted. The Mississippi Delta was not glitzy like Memphis. In fact, it was a lot like home, except that the farms were large, the homes of the landowners were stately, and the soil was black rather than red. It was the music that made these trips special. Ann's floor vibrated when she played boogey tunes like "Down Yonder" on her piano. During visits to Harvey's family farm, Ann and her sister-in-law, Helen, took turns pounding the keys of Helen's blue piano that matched the walls of her expansive bedroom.

These exploits could lead to the conclusion that growing up poor in the South of the fifties was as much fun as a Huck Finn adventure, and that is partially true. Our hard work and innovative exploits built character and imagination. The camaraderie spawned lifelong bonds of loyalty. If you are destined to grow up in financial deprivation, there are advantages to being located in the open expanse and freedom of the countryside instead of a city tenement.

The pricks of growing up in an impoverished environment didn't come from blackberry thorns or cotton burrs. They came from a childhood regularly interrupted by worry about survival. In our case, it was from knowing at a young age that the absence of letters from our father meant no funds to sustain us. From sensing Mother's desperation upon our empty-handed return from the post office. And from things as commonplace as watching her remove the heavy metal top that covered the butane tank in our yard to monitor the needle, anxiously gauging how many days the contents would last, knowing there was no money to refill it.

For several years after Daddy left, Mother managed to sustain us with the food we raised, sporadic and decreasing funds from our father, and wages earned picking cotton in the fall. She was finally forced to accept Relief, as Welfare was referred to at the time, for a few years before Betty, Tony, and Cindy started school, freeing her to go to work in Pontotoc. Even as kids, we understood the stigma of being on the dole. When Uncle Lowell delivered the commodities each month, I prayed he would come after dark so the neighbors would not see us unload the commodity cheese and peanut butter. The shame was intensified by the look on Mr. Dolan's face each month when he cashed our government check, a look that communicated without words the burden our family represented to self-sustaining people like him, the look that confirmed our second-class position even when measured against our impoverished peers. Mr. Dolan was not financially well off, but he was self-sustaining, and that afforded him the respect we could not claim. I felt ashamed. Once those seeds of shame take root, they can sprout and grow throughout one's life, popping up at the most unexpected times.

Maybe it is the feeling of being judged as less than adequate, if only by yourself, and knowing you will do everything you can to cross the invisible threshold to respectability that ties together our family's heritage with many African Americans who lived as we did, hanging on by a thread, a prayer, and the will to survive and thrive. People ask what propelled my siblings and me to succeed, after having grown up in an economically deprived environment, when so many do not escape the clutches of poverty. An important element is that a pattern of dependence on outside assistance was not established in our family. Through their words and actions, Mother, Mama and Papa made sure we knew that our acceptance of Relief was a temporary necessity but not a permanent solution. We were expected to make something of our lives, and they would have accepted no other outcome. Of no small significance is the role each sibling played in giving the next one a leg-up and by lifting each other up when the world knocked us down. Many other factors came into play, but without question, our determination to escape the shame associated with our impoverished state was a major motivator.

Children mistakenly feel responsible for their economic circumstances, and in subtle ways, adults often perpetuate that myth. The shame of being considered "less than" by others eats away at a child's spirit, and spirits are transparent, undifferentiated by race. The notion that race is the most significant issue that divides our country in the twenty-first century seems myopic when viewed from the standpoint of the striking similarities of impoverished households. The providers of healthcare and education do not grant access because an indigent person is white. Minimum wage is not adjusted based on ethnicity. The bruises inflicted by poverty are universal, and the judges of merit do not give you a pass for being fair of skin. Perhaps it is time to focus less on the differences among races and more on the commonalities of all people in need. Because nothing is easy for the children of poverty, not even the summertime.

CHRISTMAS EVE MAGIC

St. Nicholas's load was reduced by at least one household every December 24, since he never visited the Flaherty household on that particular night. That is not to say that he did not deliver a doll or a BB gun to a happy recipient in our clan, but simply that the visitation from the hearty fellow occurred on some random occasion prior to the traditionally celebrated date. This was one tradition that did not change when our father vacated the premises for his final time. Prior to his departure, he and Mother would travel to the county seat on some indeterminate December day and return with our toys. It seems the two of them frequently ran into Santa at Kuhn's dime store, where he would insist on sending, days ahead of schedule, a present for each of us kids. When the car doors swung open, the toys were distributed, be it on December 15 or December 24.

After Daddy left us, Mammaw Flaherty was faithful in sending Mother twenty-five dollars every December so that the Christmas gifts of our childhood could continue. Even in the unusual years when Mother tried to conceal the booty until the blessed day arrived, one of us would get the scent and discover her hiding place. One year, Tony and Cindy discovered their rocking horses so early in December that they just about wore them out before the presents were officially received. Strangely, in spite of all this evidence to the contrary, I clung to my belief in Santa until I was eleven years old.

In truth, Mother has never placed much stock in celebrating any occasion on the exact date, but to her credit, she still remembers the birthday of each of her nine children. Mom's card arrives early in the month of October, commemorating the anniversary of my birth on October 28. After raising eight children of her own and three grandchildren to boot, it is remarkable that she gets the cards delivered in the correct month, much less on the exact date. Mother gave birth to nine children, but her parents took quite a shine to the firstborn, Ann, and raised her as their own. Had Mother been older than sixteen at the time of Ann's birth, she would probably not have allowed that to happen. As kids, Dena and I were more than a trifle jealous of Ann, because she enjoyed many of the benefits afforded an only child. For one thing, she had a piano and learned to play it, which was a luxury in our book. She also had a bedroom of her own, rather than sleeping three or four to a room. In retrospect, hers was a lonelier life than ours, because the presence of a sibling with whom to grouse or grieve is, as MasterCard would say, priceless.

It was not unusual that the Christmas Eve afternoon when I was five, Dena and I were proudly hugging to our chests the baby dolls Santa had already delivered. When Daddy decided the two of us should spend the night with Mama and Papa, we readily agreed. We recognized that he was trying to get us out of his hair. Still, spending the night with Mama and Papa was fine with us, especially when Daddy was around. His visits caused a disruption in the order of things, what with him insisting on claiming the alpha dog position in our female household, in spite of not having lived there during our lifetimes.

Daddy did not tarry long at Mama's back screen door when he dropped us off, the enmity between the two of them being deep and long-standing. While Mama had a repertoire of adjectives to describe our father when she assumed we were out of earshot, her favorite seemed to be *sorry*. "He's a sorry excuse for a man," she'd say, with variations like, "He's a sorry excuse for a husband," or "He's a sorry excuse for a provider." She lamented rather frequently that Mother had married a Flaherty, since according to Mama, the Flahertys were a sorry lot in general and our father the sorriest of them all. In time, each of us would connect the dots and realize that as Flahertys, we were part of the sorry group to whom Mama referred, and we dreaded the day the first evidence of this trait presented itself. Our only hope seemed to lie in the small possibility that the McCord, Whitworth, and Tutor blood that coursed through our veins would produce a miracle in us. Still, I had only delightful images of Uncle Howard, Aunt Zettie Mae, and Mammaw Flaherty, none of whom seemed the least bit sorry about anything. Nor did they have any reason to be. They were among our favorite people, hard working yet fun to be around. Still, Mama was not someone you questioned, so I came to begrudgingly accept my siblings' and my sorry states. We did not understand that Mama's was merely giving voice to the prejudice against the Irish that was common among people of Scottish and English heritage.

The depth of Mama's disdain for our father was made clearer to me when, at age one hundred, her mental faculties took leave of the present and left her dwelling exclusively in the past. On one of my visits with her at the Sunshine Nursing Home, she enlightened me about her perception of Daddy's heritage, and indirectly, my own. She motioned with her finger that she had a secret she wanted to share with me, and I bent close to hear it.

"Did you know Otis is half black?" she asked in a whisper. Now my father was a dark Irishman, that much is true, but he had no features denoting an African American heritage. I went along with her just the same, wondering where this conversation was taking us.

"No, I certainly did not know that," I responded with feigned astonishment. "Tell me how you know!"

Mama crooked her forefinger for me to come even closer, so ghastly was the morsel of truth she was about to impart. "I once saw him naked," her eyes were large now, "and half his body is black. He is white from the waist up, but black from the waist down," she said, clearly proud of herself for having uncovered this truth while shaking her head in dismay at the revelation all at the same time.

It took a measure of control on my part not to burst out in laughter, so ludicrous was the mental picture she painted. Yet her description was just as a child might picture someone she perceived to be of mixed race, and I figured this was something she had visualized about someone she'd heard about in her childhood. Mama must have had questions about the purity of the Flaherty lineage because of their swarthy complexions, and given her sentiment about African Americans, that helped me to understand the origin of her disdain of our paternal bloodline.

So it is understandable that Daddy did not dawdle at Mama's back door that Christmas Eve or any other, and he was quickly backing out of the driveway and headed home. Mama treated Dena and me to orange slices and "nigger toes," the racially derogatory name for a lard and sugar candy dipped in chocolate before progressive people began to refer to the confections as chocolate drops. For Dena and me, the word held no meaning, because at that time we did know any African American people and did not understand the origin of the candy's name. As the day waned, Papa played a few carols on the piano, picking out the tunes by ear rather than reading music. Mama sat in her rocker by the old Victrola and crocheted white socks with a pink edge for Betty Jo, the newest Flaherty girl. You could always count on Mama to be busy with her hands, even when she was otherwise at rest. I never saw Mama when she was not doing something. Papa said she even worked in her sleep, and he chided her for never letting herself rest. During her last year of life when she was in a nursing home bed, she constantly moved her hands as though she was knitting or sewing. I took her some scraps, thread, and a needle, and she seemed to find some relief in pushing the needle through the cloth.

In keeping with the ways of Mississippi farmers in those days, we were tucked into bed by seven that night. We had not been in bed long when a car's lights penetrated the thick darkness that perpetually surrounded Mama and Papa's home place at night. They lived so far out in the country that once Dena inquired of them whether the moon shone that far out. Mama got a real kick out of that question and told her that on occasion it made its way to their remote location.

Nestled in our beds, we heard a car door slam. We were at first anxious, since cars rarely found their way up Papa's driveway after dark. For an instant, I held a glimmer of hope that Santa was making a second delivery on our behalf to this location, arriving by car instead of sleigh. That illusion was shattered when someone knocked on the front door, an action unnecessary for Santa Claus. It scared me that someone had knocked on the door so late at night since family members would have yelled out their names or come right on in through the unlocked door.

Papa pulled on his overalls and opened the door without hesitation. A man's voice inquired of him whether he performed marriages, having identified the notation of reverend on the mailbox down by the road. Papa told him he did, and the man said that he and his fiancée wanted to be married right away. Papa asked to see the license, and when the visitor produced one, Papa told the gentleman and his lady friend to have a seat in the living room while he and Mama prepared properly for a wedding.

Imagine how quickly Dena's and my feet hit the lino-leum floor, given that we were not only about to attend our first wedding but a Christmas Eve nuptial to boot! While Papa changed into a starched white shirt and dark trousers, Mama put on a Sunday dress. Of course, we could not attend a wedding in pajamas, so we slipped into our Christmas frocks. Mama selected a white coco-nut cake from the several cakes she had baked for the following day's meal, and put it in the center of the din-ing room table, atop the pretty white table cloth that covered the pink and gray Formica table. She decorat-ed the cake with orange slices on the top, then set out bowls of candy and even used her special green glass dishes. There was already a Christmas tree in the living room for decoration, and Mama covered the mantel with hand-stitched doilies to create a fitting backdrop for the ceremony. Her red and clear glass vases were placed on the doilies, creating a rather elegant setting. It seems that, if you were a preacher's wife in those days, you were prepared for unexpected ceremonies from drop-in clientele, thus accounting for the ease with which she transformed the house into a fitting wedding chapel.

The man told Papa he and his bride-to-be had dated for several years but had never set a wedding date. That night, riding down the road and spotting a reverend's house, they'd decided the time was right. That scenario was almost too romantic for me to bear, though Dena and I agreed it would have been a lot better if she had worn a white gown instead of a blue dress. It was clear to Dena and me that the couple had procrastinated almost too long before taking the plunge, since they appeared to be quite mature and not exactly our idea of the ideal couple. They had to be in their mid-twenties. Still, it was a wedding and we supposed you are never too old to fall in love.

I was able to get past the inappropriateness of the participants' ages and dress as the seriousness of the ceremony to which we were parties sunk in. In particular, Papa asked them did they promise to love, honor, and obey (oh, yes, obey was in his version of the marriage ceremony) until death did them part. I didn't think that would be very long, given their advanced ages. After they agreed to a lifetime commitment, Papa rewarded them by not only allowing but actually encouraging the groom to kiss the bride. Now, that was worth the wait, getting to see them kiss right in front of us.

Mama invited the newlyweds into the dining room for a small reception, and Dena and I were permitted to drink out of the fine glass cups just like the adults. The groom paid Papa two dollars for his services, and I guess Mama's were thrown in for free. They did not linger long, because they said they still had thirty miles to travel to get home. After they left, Mama cleaned up the dining room and put away all the wedding finery, keeping it fresh for the next pair that would call upon Papa to perform a ceremony. Papa and Mama hung up their nice clothes, and we all redressed for a night of dreams.

Long after the married couple had departed for their honeymoon down in Calhoun City, Dena and I lay awake whispering about this, our most exciting Christmas Eve ever. In a way, it was like the Christmas story, where everyone's tucked in their beds and a clatter on the roof propels them into an adventure. Ours was not a clatter on the rooftop, nor was St. Nicholas part of the festivities, but since he never visited us on Christmas Eve anyway, we could not have expected him to be. This was even better. It was just like magic.

That was not the last Christmas wedding Papa performed in his and Mama's living room. James and Marie were married there on Christmas Day a few years later. How the first Christmas nuptial turned out, I do not know, but I can attest that after almost fifty years of the ups and downs, joys and tribulations that go with marriage, James and Marie are still in love. Papa would be proud that the vows they repeated after him so long ago took so well. But then, magic can happen at Christmas if only you believe!

STORMY WEATHER

I find few things to be more comforting than severely threatening weather. From the moment the warning from the National Weather Service flitters across the bottom of the TV screen, I enter a Zen state of mind. While any weather alert produces a sense of well-being, thunderstorm warnings are my favorite. The most enjoyable places I have ridden out a rainstorm were a screened porch in Alabama and a car on a New Mexico mesa, but the top of a New York skyscraper and a cottage on the Alabama gulf have proven to be fine substitutes.

Having grown up in the South, it is not a lack of experience with the ravages that can be inflicted by strong winds and rain, nor a particularly ghoulish nature that makes me find unrest in the elements to be irresistible. In fact, I suspect it is my extensive history with storms that causes me to seek refuge as close to the source as possible, a place that allows me to feel the energy without getting soaked. I came by this fiendish obsession honestly. It started with our mother, who doesn't just enjoy storms—she craves them. Her face lights up each time she advises us that the weatherman predicts turbulent weather. This is especially strange when you consider that when we were children, Mother's fear of storms resulted in hundreds of sleepless nights as we sought shelter from them.

The weathered condition of the unpainted boards covering the exterior of our small turn-of-the-century house spoke volumes about the number of storms the old place had survived. Yet Mother was certain each one would be the last. Other than a few pieces of rusted tin that blew off the roof occasionally, producing some bothersome leaks until new pieces could be nailed back into place, the house was fully intact. Nevertheless, one or two nights a week from March through June, Mother's fear for the stability of our dwelling had us traipsing back and forth between our beds and the storm cellar in Miz Flora Tutor's front yard, about one hundred yards down the road. A clap of thunder so far in the distance you had to strain to hear it resulted in another night of treks up and down the blacktop road that connected our houses.

It is difficult to blame Mother for tenaciously trying to get a head start on the storms. After all, a passel of us kids had to be sufficiently roused from sleep to dress ourselves and begrudgingly wander to our neighbor's storm cellar. When we lived behind the Grubbs family, we shared their storm cellar, and after we moved to Randolph proper, we took shelter with the Tutors. Some of us were sound sleepers, and it took a while for us to grasp the urgency Mother felt and then to get our limbs to respond. Factor in the fact that by the time each of us reached the age of five, we had experienced so many false starts we no longer felt the intensity of alarm our mother expected. Even when we tried to accommodate, our sleepiness made it difficult. Like the time James stepped into the arms of his jacket and pulled it snugly to his waist before he realized his error. He then spent so much time dislodging his legs from the jacket's narrow sleeves that the storm passed over before we left our house. The rest of us were beholden to James for his dressing error.

We must have been a sight, filing out of the house at all hours of the night, sometimes two or three times a night during the spring and summer storm season, with hair sticking out in all directions, shoes on the wrong feet, clothes piled on top of pajamas, and grousing with every step. Inevitably there was a straggler, though the person bringing up the rear alternated, depending on the mood and sleep level from which we were awakened. A bolt of lightning frequently jarred that one's gait, propelling her to pass the rest of the nomads in pursuit of safety.

No matter when we arrived at the storm cellar, Miz Flora's son, Max, would be standing outside surveying the weather, greeting us with details of the atmospheric pressure and other conditions in language we could not have understood even had we been lucid. Max, a bachelor and civil engineer who lived with his mother and his unmarried sister, was the only college-educated man in our vicinity, other than teachers at the local school. Each storm brought a welcome opportunity for him to discuss ideas and facts about which I had never thought, could scarcely conceive of, and did not care to consider. He was the first intellectual I ever knew. He watched the skies for signs of storms with the same zeal displayed by our mother, but with joyful anticipation rather than with trepidation. Had there been any apparent chemistry between them, we would have accused our mother of using these occasions to promote a tryst with the young Mr. Tutor, but even to young romantics, that was unfathomable. One simply could not envision someone who was attracted to our father also being infatuated with Max.

Most women who lived out in the country had been toughened by lives without soft edges, but Miz Flora was more formidable than other female neighbors. Her husband died soon after we moved to Randolph, and she assumed responsibility for running the place so that Max could continue his education and her daughter, Bobbie Faye, could pursue her career at the telephone company in Oxford. Miz Flora was a happy participant in the storm shelter experience, leading Max into the dungeon, she with her kerosene lantern and he with his flashlight, scouting for uninvited creatures, such as snakes that might have found the cool concrete floor or hard wood seats too inviting to resist. Miz Flora was undeterred at the prospect of facing a viper. It didn't matter how many times the two of them investigated the pit and proclaimed the cubicle reptile-free—all night long I felt the fangs poised to strike my legs and feet.

The Flaherty kids did not go quietly into that dark chamber. We stood next to the road counting the seconds between lightning strikes with the goal of staying outside until there was a one-second intermission between the two. This meant the storm was five miles away, or at least, that was what our intelligentsia Max Tutor told us. After we lingered as long as we dared outside the storm cellar and after Mother had issued a stern proclamation that she was through tolerating any more of our foolishness, we filed into the bowels of the earth with the demeanor of those poor souls summoned into the gas chambers. The shelter was a small hole in the side of a hill, dank with a smell of mold and earth. The walls of brick and cement, about four feet high, were cold to the touch, and the wooden planks used for seating offered no comfort. The structure was six feet by six feet, and about four feet in height, so that the adults had to bend at the waist to enter. During the winter, most folks stored their canned goods inside these fortresses, but come April, we were the ones packed inside as tightly as the canned goods.

Whatever enthusiasm the Flaherty children lacked for being crammed inside the snake pit, Mrs. Flora and Max more than made up for. This was their opportunity to talk to a captive audience, and that is just what they did. Max shared with us many aspects of civil engineering and other topics that Mother and my siblings, particularly Cindy and James, found fascinating. Miz Flora chimed in with apparent knowledge about James' profession that must have come from their daily exchanges. I found the subject matter to be as exciting as watching grass grow.

Max, a true Southern gentleman, periodically left the safety of the shelter to check on the storm's status, a duty I deeply coveted since it freed him from the confines of our little chamber of horrors, albeit briefly. He invariably returned with admonitions that the worst was not over and that we should stay put. How much of that information was objective is debatable, since he always returned eager to further enlighten us about Mississippi's roads and bridges. Sometimes he would report having heard a sound akin to a train passing overhead, and we'd hunker down for what we assumed was a tornado spinning through the skies above us. We were not allowed to leave immediately when the sound stopped, because there could be others in line, sort of like airplanes waiting in line to taxi out on a runway.

Eventually, when the prognostication was that it was safe for us to leave the storm shelter, we emerged from the pit and walked home through torrents of rain soaking our clothes, hair, and skin. Because our treks to the cellar generally preceded the storm's actual arrival, we made the first half of the trip completely dry. Once the worst part of the storm was over, the rain could continue for hours, leaving us no alternative but to return home through a downpour. It seemed illogical to us kids that we left the warmth of our beds to go for a walk in dry weather, sit in a moldy cellar for a few hours, return through a downpour, and arrive back at our house soaking wet and tired. As we surfaced from the crypt, we immediately looked up the road to see if our house had withstood the storm, and upon confirming that it had, lambasted our mother with multiple "I told you sos."

Ironically, the house survived until we moved away, and when it eventually did meet its demise, it was the element of fire, not wind, that destroyed it.

Equally ironically, we stayed home during the worst storm to pass through North Mississippi prior to Hurricane Camille. In 1957, Hurricane Audrey wreaked havoc along the Louisiana coast and followed a path up through Mississippi, maintaining ravaging winds. How Audrey managed to catch both my mother and Max Tutor off guard is still a mystery. She roared into Randolph in the middle of the night, with gale force winds sufficient to uproot an oak tree that had stood in our yard for more than one hundred years and to blow a smaller one onto our rooftop. When the sound awoke me, I discovered Mother sitting in the kitchen, watching the window fan's blades spin at high speed. I asked her why she had turned on the fan in the middle of a storm. Our situation became clear to me when she told me the fan was not plugged in.

The winds roared, and we were at the storm's mercy for what seemed like hours. Having missed our opportunity to travel safely to the storm cellar, all we could do was watch and pray. In the midst of the storm, everything quieted down for a moment, and the worst seemed to be over. Then the force of the gale returned, fiercer than before.

The power of that storm was palpable, and it had us firmly in its grip. Somehow that realization both terrified and comforted me simultaneously, as for the first time, I sensed a truth that has been reinforced through the years. When you completely lose control and accept your defenselessness, a kind of peace settles over you. At those times, your fate is clearly up to God.

After the winds and rain subsided, our old house was still standing along with the others in our community, and no one in our vicinity was injured. In terms of human life, God was good to Randolph that night, though not so kind to those in Louisiana, where some six hundred people lost their lives as the June hurricane caught them unprepared.

I'm not sure if our failure to take shelter during this most threatening storm was the reason, but soon thereafter, Papa dug us a shelter of our own beside our house so that the tour down the road was not necessary. Actually, there was relatively little digging to be done, since my siblings and I had been excavating that spot every summer for years with the goal of creating an in-ground swimming pool. Our storm cellar was earthen rather than brick, making it more susceptible to snakes. Strangely, I missed being regaled by Miz Flora and Max's stories. Maybe because Mother also did not quite trust the new cellar or because she figured if our house survived Hurricane Audrey, it could survive any storm, she sought shelter in the below-ground sanctuary less and less frequently during my last few years at home. She began to accept storms, and eventually, her aversion to them morphed into a passion.

It is interesting how differently we perceived the storm shelter, with Cindy seeing it as a safe haven and me as a snake pit, and how our reactions to the threat of storms vary in adulthood. Most of us feel safest when it storms, and we prefer to observe rather than escape their fury. My sisters and I agree our perception of safety during storms stems from another aspect of our childhoods. The absence of a man in our home produced vulnerability to invasion, and as kids, we thought no one would subject himself to harsh elements just to break into our house. Only Ann and Bobby maintain vigils during foul weather, taking shelter well before an alarm sounds. As punishment for poking fun at their heightened weather-related concerns, I may someday be blown from my upstairs bedroom by a tornado's force. In the meantime, I will have enjoyed many good, dry nights' sleep to the melodious rumble of thunder.

GUARDIAN ANGELS

About ten years ago, Cindy gave each of her four sisters a cherished gift for Christmas: a painting of a guardian angel guiding two small children across a rickety bridge. The young travelers are seemingly unaware of the celestial presence shepherding them to safety. The significance of this gift is that a smaller version of this picture graced our living room wall throughout our youth. Because we lived in immaculate but austere surroundings, that picture was one of two in our home. It served as a reminder that, like those two children, we were protected by an unseen force.

The story of how the original picture came to be in our home made Cindy's gift to us even more significant. One day, a visitor to my third grade class announced a contest designed to encourage thirty children, eight-to-ten-year-olds, to sell pictures of birds in order to win the coveted top prize of a white leather-bound Bible with gold leaf lettering on the cover and Jesus' words printed in red italics in the inner text. Much can be said about the rural Mississippi culture that fostered children who would work so hard to receive a copy of the scriptures, but in 1958, a Bible was still considered a prized possession. The pictures were the most colorful I had ever seen, with brilliantly red cardinals, dazzling blue birds, and vivid black and white wood peckers with their contrasting red heads. An azure sky was the backdrop for each image.

So it was that one Sunday afternoon, after exhausting all the sales opportunities in our tiny, impoverished community, and two sales short of the ten necessary to earn the coveted Bible, I became desperate. The money collected from the sales had to be turned in the following day. It was cold, rainy, and gray, and still I concluded that branching out into the adjacent community two miles away down Highway 9 was my only hope of achieving my goal. Anticipating what Mother's answer would be, I implored her to allow me to walk down the new road to the Carey Springs community. I was sure that in that cluster of houses just down that highway, the would-be owner of a brightly painted woodpecker and cardinal awaited my arrival. My desire to own the beautifully bound edition of the gospel had turned into an obsession strong enough to propel me to brave the elements for one last shot at it.

This is where my memory produces two scenarios: the one I want to have happened and the one I know in my heart is real. In the first scenario, a man agrees with Mother that it is too cold and dreary for a young child to venture out alone, but he has an alternative to which I am unaccustomed. He says he will take me to the adjacent community in his car. In our world, we seldom rode in an automobile, except on those rare occasions when our father came home from Memphis and took us on one of our ill-fated family outings. I feel an ache in my chest when I imagine this male ransoming my dream, because in my other childhood memories, princes did not ride in to rescue my siblings, our mother, or me. The voice is distinctively male, and through the process of elimination, I deduce it must belong to my father. This possibility is incongruent with other memories of my father, so as I ponder it, I phone Dena to ask if she, another keeper of our family memories, remembers who took me to sell the remaining pictures. She agrees that if I went by car, it must have been Daddy, as improbable as that seems.

This much is true. The sales came through. Colored bird prints brightened Miz Ila Douglas's kitchen walls for years to come. Yet going to school the next day to claim my prize, my spirits were devoid of the elation I should have felt. Daddy was leaving us again, and based on a conversation Dena and I overheard between him and our mother, this time would be different from the others. He was not coming back. He suggested placing all the children who were still at home in an orphanage, so that he and mother could start over somewhere else unencumbered by five little urchins. Cindy was still a baby, Tony not quite two, and Betty Jo would turn four the following May. In his plan, I am not sure what would have become of Larry, away in Jackson at the Mississippi School for the Deaf. Ann, Bobby, and James were on their own by then, so they were not part of the equation.

At eleven, Dena was sufficiently mature to grasp the gravity of the situation and was beside herself with fear at the prospect of our having to leave home and be separated from one another. I, on the other hand, always ready to go some place, any place, pointed out to her that an orphanage might not be that bad. "After all," I encouraged her, "we've never been to an orphanage." Or much of anywhere else for that matter. That Pollyanna-like response has been the source of heckling all my life. My inclination to insist on seeing the brighter side of a dilemma is a trait that Dena finds irritating at best. Each time I point out the positive angle, Dena responds sarcastically, "And we've never been to an orphanage, either."

The issue was moot. Mother refused to leave us, and instead, she accompanied Daddy to the First National

Bank of Pontotoc to secure a loan, pledging our home as collateral. The plan was that he would use the money to get a new start and then send for us to join him at some nebulous future date. Hence, the lyrics of one of the Temptations' songs, "All He Left Us Was Alone" resonated with us, although for us it was "All He Left Us Was Alone and a Loan." True to form, he did not send for us or provide the money to repay the debt. Every year or two after that, emboldened by a few drinks, Daddy called Mother to say he was buying a beautiful home and would be in touch soon with details of how we would reunite. On one of these occasions, he provided those details, telling Mother he had purchased a three-bedroom, one-bath home in Capleville, a suburb of Memphis. Before Christmas break, my siblings and I obtained our school records in preparation for the family's relocation. Our phone fell silent, and we returned to our school that January, gravely disappointed and chagrined.

True to his word, Daddy did return. Nine years later while my siblings and I were at school, he walked up to our house, sat down in a straight chair on the front porch, and tilted it back, as nonchalant as if he had strolled up to Larry Onsby's store and had stayed a little longer than he had planned. There were no words of explanation. He had simply come back home. That day, Mother sent him away…alone.

The Monday of Daddy's initial departure was also the day the children who had sold their quota of bird paintings received their prizes. Unfortunately, the winners outnumbered the available Bibles. Apparently, the promoters underestimated the religious fervor of their sales representatives. Consequently, the third grade class was advised that some of us would win the alternate award, a picture of an angel guiding two small children safely across a rotted wooden bridge with treacherous gaps between the planks. Its message of protection by an unseen force became pivotal in our household.

Years later, I mentally painted a scenario whereby my father facilitated the sale of the last two bird pictures, and consequently, was responsible for the symbol that graced our walls. I created a personal myth that upon his final parting, Daddy left us a reminder of his protection, guiding us through danger from afar, an indication of his well-hidden love and concern for us. Taken to its logical conclusion, I further deduced that our father, through this parting gift, conveyed to his children our own wings, wings that permitted us to fly, to leave our nest knowing we never fly alone. A sort of guardian angel in absentia.

It would be wonderful if that was how it all happened, would it not? However, there is a contradictory version of this story that invades my consciousness, and it has all the earmarks of being accurate. It is true that a car was parked in our driveway, but in the alternate recollection of that afternoon, I did not ride in it. In this account, I can feel my limbs, rigid from the cold, as I walk the two miles to the Carey Springs community, moving quickly to finish the hike before the early darkness descends. I am accompanied by someone who, upon hearing of my dilemma, left a warm, comfortable house, gave up his one afternoon of rest for the week, and walked two miles from his house to ours to fetch me back down to his neighborhood. In my mind's eye, I see him waiting patiently beside each mailbox while I make my spiel and sell the remaining pictures. Then he walked me home before retracing his steps back to his warm abode. This memory carries the ring of truth.

A real-life guardian angel accompanied me that afternoon, the same one who came every Monday to start a fire under the black iron pot where Mother and Mama washed our clothes. The one who ransomed our house from foreclosure when Daddy did not repay the loan. The man who, a few years later, would sell his and Mama's one-hundred-acre farm to Uncle Lowell at a significantly reduced rate, give Aunt Louella her share of the proceeds, and use Mother's share to add a room to our house and cover the rotting wooden exterior with asbestos siding.

Daddy's absence gave him a larger-than-life presence. We did not speak of him because the mention of his name visibly upset Mother, but our silence only exaggerated his significance. As children, we dreamed in vain of a father who would care for us. While we dreamed that a protector would appear, the purveyor of the guardianship symbol on our wall was consistently in our midst, shielding us. Thank you, Papa, for guarding us so faithfully while our eyes looked past you in an unending search for an elusive protector.

ESCAPE ROUTES

E scape can take many forms, and running away is not always a physical act. There are myriad ways to vacate the premises. My first physical escape was poorly executed. I made my maiden journey at age six or seven when my feelings were wounded by what I perceived as Mother's failure to adequately appreciate the gift of my presence in her life. Gathering just a few things together, since I had no intention of going farther or staying longer than it took to scare the beejesuz out of Mother, I trod less than one hundred yards into the adjoining pasture before taking refuge beside an extinct pond on Miz Flora's property. In retrospect, my hiding place was clearly visible from Mother's vantage point. Still, I counted on the tall cattails growing rampantly on the pond's bank to provide cover for my small body. It was a late winter day, almost spring, but with a lingering chill. Languishing among the brown and tan undergrowth and warmed by the sun, it was not an unpleasant location … for the first thirty minutes or so. In those early moments, I waited with gleeful heart for Mother to call my name in a voice filled with terror and regret, having discovered that I had taken my leave.

As the sun's rays waned and I was forced to migrate around the pond to stay warm, the reality dawned that I was going to have to go inside without my absence having been noticed. Within an hour from the time I had so determinedly trudged to the pond, I was plodding back to the house, hungry and beaten down by the harsh reality of life out in the world. Mother turned to me as I entered the kitchen and said, "So you're back. I saw you hiding in the weeds." Bummer! Not only had my departure not driven her to madness, she had known my location all the time I had been gone. Next time, I vowed I would plan my escape more carefully, take some provisions so that I could travel farther—at least out of eyesight.

As our family life began to deteriorate, my escapes took a different tack, shifting from physical to mental. When things became uncomfortable, I learned to slip away as easily as flipping off a light switch. In the midst of an unpleasant situation, I would change the channel and be transported to somewhere more exotic. After discovering llamas in my third grade geography book, Peru became a favorite place to visit. When puberty hit, travel to other countries was replaced by fantasy encounters with boys who were transfixed by my beauty and charm. Oh! The boys I left adrift in my wake. Flights of imagination allow a person to momentarily escape many unpleasant realities. Maybe life's early experiences are designed to teach us behaviors that will be useful later in life. Life holds some experiences that can best be managed when one is not fully present.

At age twelve, just as my girlfriends were being visited by menses, heralding their transition into womanhood, I was discovering blood in a less expected place—in my urine. This was a sufficiently significant event to warrant a rare trip to a physician in Pontotoc. Most injuries and illnesses were treated with home remedies. A potato poltice, consisting of an uncooked Irish potato ground to the consistency of a paste and held in place by a strip of muslin tightly bound, could cure almost anything. For folks living in the country, visits to the doctor were generally limited to incidences of broken limbs other than fingers and toes (those were set at home), some but not all child births, and bush hogging accidents that severed a body part. After examining me and taking a urine specimen, the doctor diagnosed my symptoms as a manifestation of a rather severe kidney infection, which he treated with a round of sulfur tablets and a strict warning to eat and drink a good deal when the tablets were administered.

These bouts of pain in the lower back became a routine part of my life, occurring every few weeks for the next four years. Mother and several of my siblings had periodic kidney infections, so we assumed that my condition was the same as theirs. A sulfur drug provided by Uncle Lowell was taken if all other home remedies failed. Usually, the pain in my side could be reduced by hot compresses, or in the wintertime, by lying on the floor in front of the butane heater with the heat penetrating my skin. Often, neither the heat nor the turpentine mixture rubbed on the skin did any good, and the pain would continue unabated for several days. It was during those periods that my mental flights took on new dimensions. One day while lying on the bed wondering if I would be able to bear the pain another moment, I became transfixed by the birds sitting on the telephone line outside the window. For some reason, those birds seemed to offer me a ticket to freedom. I imagined how it would feel to fly away with them, leaving the pain behind. Just for a moment, I mentally did that. From that day forward, I knew I could handle the discomfort, because I had learned how to leave it behind for a few moments at a time.

Mother remained unaware of the severity of my condition. Aside from the fact that she was struggling to keep us fed and clothed while coping with her own emotional malaise, I admit to being an accomplice in her denial. I hid much of my pain from her, believing she had enough to worry about. It was also in my self-interest to keep her in the dark. Mother's solution to my pain predictably involved confinement to bed, missing school, and refraining from any activity as taxing as playing basketball or cheerleading. There was no way I would forego the best things life in the remote countryside had to offer just because I was sick. So it was that the extent of my problems went undetected until the morning of the dress rehearsal for our junior class play, *Aaron Slick from Possum Crick*. The girls in our first-period home economics class were giggling excitedly as we preened in front of the mirror, preparing for the re-hearsal, when suddenly I was no longer standing but on the floor, crawling around and emitting sounds reminis-cent of a dog howling. Our home-ec teacher and second-cousin, Doris, sent for the principal, Mr. Hood, and within minutes I was loaded into his automobile and transported to the emergency room at the Pontotoc County Hospital. We made a quick stop at Uncle Lowell's drug store, where Mother worked six days a week, and she rode with us to the hospital. When the doctor gave us his preliminary diagnosis of appendicitis, Mother's eyes and mine exchanged a silent message. Her eyes said, "Dear Lord, How are we ever going to pay for something that involves surgery?" to which mine replied, "I'm so sorry to have caused this problem."

The doctor turned out to be wrong. A battery of X-rays revealed the culprit to be not a ruptured appendix but seven rather large stones lodged in my kidneys. Apparently, they had been there a long time, because they had wreaked havoc on the left kidney, which was three times its normal size, and had caused some damage to the right. Alternatively, my left kidney might have been deformed since birth and the malfunction might have caused an infection from which the stones formed. The doctor was unsure about the origin of the problem, but he *was* sure that the necessary surgery was beyond the realm of any local surgeon. I was immediately referred to the Baptist Medical Center in Memphis.

This news was troublesome on a number of fronts. The seriousness of my condition could no longer be swept aside. Also, our family places a lot of stock in dreams and other psychic messages, and just a few weeks prior, I had told Mother about a dream I'd had. The dream had been ominous, so I made it a point to tell someone about it before I ate breakfast. Superstition held that if you told a dream before breakfast, it would not come true. The dream I shared with Mother took place in a very large facility with lots of hallways teeming with men in long white coats. The men were quite serious and walked purposefully. It seemed as though I had been there a long time, and one of them told me I might not ever leave the facility. Just as I was becoming anxious, a man with black hair and dark-rimmed glasses appeared, looked me in the eyes, and told me I was going be okay. Either because Mother discerned the impact this dream had on me or because of her own gift of precognition, she did not scoff at my reaction. Perhaps a scientifically oriented person would say my unconscious mind was merely acknowledging my declining physical condition, which was pretty effectively ignored by day. Given our predilection for the supernatural, it comes as no surprise that the latter interpretation did not occur to my mother or to me

Five days after the episode at school, Mother and I arrived at the Baptist Memorial Hospital. Betty, Tony and Cindy stayed in Randolph with Dena. Mama and Papa could not provide their usual assistance, because Papa was not well himself, suffering from as yet undiagnosed pancreatic cancer that would take his life two months later. I can remember minute details from childhood but cannot recall our mode of transportation to Memphis that day. I do recall a sense of dread wondering how the people in charge of the hospital would react when they learned we had no ability to pay for their services. My anxiety was heightened when we were escorted to a brand-new wing and assigned to a semi-private room, complete with a television mounted on the wall and a telephone placed on a stand between the two beds. These accommodations were clearly beyond our means. Then again, any room in the hospital would have been.

In 1966, hospital administrators did not subject patients to the hours-long admission ordeal of modern-day health care. In a much more civilized but less revenue-enhancing manner, after you were comfortably settled in your room and given a meal, a pleasant person came by to inquire about your payment method. The look on the woman's face when Mother told her we had no insurance and no money to make even a down payment confirmed my suspicion that a mistake had been made. I was definitely in the wrong bed. The woman left the room without saying much more. In the meantime, we were visited by a man in a long white coat who informed us he would be my doctor. Something was definitely amiss. The doctor had light-colored hair and did not even wear glasses.

Not much time elapsed before an attendant I would later learn was called an orderly arrived with a wheelchair. He explained that I had been assigned to the wrong room and that he would take us to the appropriate floor. Subsequently, I have observed that if you are a sane, paying patient, you are told you will be staying in room number x, but if you are indigent or mentally disturbed, you are simply assigned to a designated floor or unit. In this case, that floor was the basement of an annex that had been part of the original hospital before a bright, shiny new one had been erected adjacent to it. Unlike the cheerful, sun-filled rooms and shiny beige tile floors in the replacement wing, this one had dark brown linoleum and a shortage of windows. We were taken to a ward housing thirteen beds, six on the left and seven on the right, with adequate space in the middle for medical personnel to push carts, wheelchairs, and gurneys. It was my first coed experience, and I was junior to the other residents by a range of twenty to sixty years. It was my good fortune that the bed beside the door, bed number one, was vacant. The room had one window at the opposite end, but it was located too high for the patients to see much of anything, which was just as well since our building was sandwiched between two taller ones.

As strange as it sounds, my spirits lifted as soon as we were settled in the bowels of that little building. It was old, worn, and dark, with only a single phone located in the nurses' station. The beds had seen their better days, having been discarded when replacements were ordered for the new hospital. These quarters felt more like home. While we could not afford to pay for care in this unit, either, it did not feel so far out of our league. In addition, I figured we had a much better chance of repaying the hospital for the cost of my care here than in the nicer, modern section.

I soon realized the Indigent Care Unit hardly needed windows when it had Dorothy Wilson. Dorothy was a nurse's aide par excellence. When she entered the unit, the sunshine came in with her. She was a pretty African American woman in her late thirties or early forties, with skin the color of café mocha that smelled of Lady Esther face cream and Jergen's hand lotion, scents that were particularly endearing to me because they were the same brands Mother used. I knew from our first encounter that I would come to love the woman who lit up Baptist Memorial Hospital's charity ward.

Not only had my bed assignment changed, a different physician was assigned to my case. As the teaching hospital for the University of Tennessee Medical School, Baptist Memorial Hospital was the training ground for interns and residents. My case was given to a resident named Dr. DiBandi. As soon as I met him, all my fears were allayed. He was a small man who somewhat resembled Mr. Peepers, a television character played by Wally Cox. The large black-rimmed glasses on his small face were almost comical. I thought, *"So this is the doctor who is going to make everything okay?" You have got to be kidding!*

One of the difficult things about being in a ward was that visitors were permitted only during visiting hours, and under no circumstance was anyone allowed to stay overnight with a patient, even on the night following surgery. The RNs, in their stiff white uniforms and caps with just one thin black line to connote their senior position relative to other members of the nursing staff, monitored body intake of intravenous antibiotics and glucose as well as the output of urine through a catheter emptying into a clear bag tied to the bed rail. Throughout the night, people dressed in white came into the ward to take vial after vial of blood from multiple patients, flipping on the overhead florescent lights as they entered the door. It was the nurse's aides, dressed in pink, who answered our calls about discomfort and who brought us a small carton of ice cream and its accompanying wooden spoon just before lights out. Dorothy was everyone's favorite of those angels of mercy.

Mother arrived daily between six thirty and seven in the morning with James or Bobby, depending on where she had spent the night. The brother who brought Mother would come in and visit for a few minutes before heading to work, and the one taking her to his house that night would stop by to say hello. I cherished Mother's presence, having her to myself in a way I had not since early childhood. She was both physically and mentally present with me. When the fevers raged, she cooled my parched lips with pieces of ice, and on days when surgery was to be performed late in the day, slipped one chip of ice into my dry mouth in spite of the restrictions against liquids being ingested prior to surgery.

Making everything okay turned out not to be an easy feat for Dr. DiBandi. After two non-invasive surgeries to remove the stones, one stubborn formation remained lodged in the left kidney, blocking the ureter. Following the third surgery, the nurses jokingly told me I would no longer be able to wear a bikini, and once I saw the incision that went halfway around my rapidly shrinking waist line, I concluded they were right. At sixteen, a girl's perception of her appearance changes when she has too many pimples. An eight-inch scar around the midsection takes more getting used to. Symmetry has always been important to me, yet I would not have been comforted to know that in a couple of years, an equivalent scar on the right side would bring my body back into balance.

At that time, cosmetic concerns were secondary. An operation the next week to correct the cause of urine reflux into my left kidney was unsuccessful, and my condition was worsening. Additional X-rays with fish dye inserted into my veins allowed the radiologists to watch the kidney's function. It was slow to process liquids and the blockage in the ureter pushed the urine back into the kidney. Dr. DiBandi said he had to repair the ureter, which had either been damaged by the passage of stones or had been deformed since birth, causing the original problems with the kidney.

After the fourth surgery my condition plummeted. Those are the days I cannot recall, except snippets of being bathed in ice water to lower my spiking temperature. By then I had been in the hospital for three weeks, and my weight had declined from one hundred and seven to ninety pounds. My prognosis was written on Dr. DiBandi's face. I wanted to reassure him it would be okay. Not only had the dream told me that, Jesus whispered it into my ear every day.

Eventually, my fever climbed so high that even the baths in ice and alcohol had little effect. At that juncture, Dr. DiBandi confided to Mother that he honestly did not know what to do. He was concerned I might be too weak to survive another surgery, but if he did not operate death was inevitable. Concluding that the risk of doing nothing was greater, he operated again, this time inserting a simulated ureter. Mother told me that when he brought me back to the room, he would not allow the orderly to remove me from the gurney. Dr. DiBandi personally lifted me with utmost care and placed me on my bed. When Mother told me about this, I wished I could have seen the care that sounded so fatherly.

That night and the next, the unit violated its rule about no visitors after 8:30 p.m. I guess they could not bear to see a young girl die alone. Mother sat all night in the waiting room, allowed to come into the ward only for a few minutes every couple of hours. Then a medical miracle occurred, and the third day after surgery, I rebounded. Two days later, Mother was brushing my hair when a RN stuck her head around the cloth room divider. Seeing that my condition had turned a corner, she teased me that the nurses had started a poll about whether I would make it or not and congratulated me for beating the odds. You recover quickly when you are young. One week after the final surgery, with Mother supporting my eighty-five-pound frame and me lugging a transparent bag filled with my urine, we emerged from the dark hallway into a sunny April day.

It would take eight years, multiple surgeries, and ultimately a left nephrectomy to permanently free me of stones and recurrent attacks, and another ten years before my urologist, Dr. Comfort (aptly named), could stop prescribing the daily antibiotics required to clear the right kidney of infection. During that time, I left no stone unturned in my quest for healing, including having hands laid on me by a Pentecostal preacher and other faith healers.

This untreated childhood condition took another toll on my life. Against the doctors' advice, I became pregnant during the first year of my marriage to my second husband, Dennis. Early in the pregnancy, problems arose. After a battery of test, the doctors advised us that my damaged kidney could not support the fetus and me, and possibly not either one of us. They concluded that a therapeutic abortion must be performed in order to save my life. Although the doctors did not present their findings as debatable, it was an agonizing decision for me and a painful reality for Dennis. After the pregnancy was terminated, I elected to have my tubes tied to avoid ever again having to choose between my own life and that of my unborn child. So it was that Dennis and I, two people who loved children so much, met our need for their presence by spending considerable time with the adorable nieces and nephews our sisters and brothers unselfishly shared with us. Then one day in 1985, our adoption request came through and another person's baby became our own. Ryan escaped from foster care into our open arms.

Had our father not chosen to escape his responsibility as a parent, I might have received the medical care I needed and my life would have been different. Just as some say that even a butterfly flapping its wings in Asia creates an imperceptible change in America, every person's escape creates a ripple effect through the lives of others. If healthcare had been an equal right for every person regardless of the ability to pay, Mother would have made sure I was taken to a doctor before the damage occurred. Maybe the change my illness created was negative. Maybe it was positive. I do not know. I do know it resulted in the greatest gift I have ever received, my son Ryan. As Dena reminds me, we do not know where the road to the life we did not live would have led or when and how it would have ended.

For most of my life, my illness was something from which I sought to escape and to ostracize from my life, refusing to let it define who I would become. I like to believe that God and the universe provide what we need to develop our character. It is passé to say the weakness in my body made my core strong and prepared me not to give up no matter what challenge life threw my way. It also may be true that it took a major setback to balance my self-directed personality with the humility essential to become a compassionate person. The fact that I am now healthy leads me to believe in miracles. Sometimes miracles are slow in coming, and an escape route comes in handy. Whatever it takes, it is important to stay the course. As Tony often advised, "Don't give up before the miracle happens!"

GIVE ME THAT OLD TIME RELIGION

From the time our little legs would support our bodies, every Sunday morning you could find Mother's kids running up and down the pews of the Carey Springs Missionary Baptist Church sanctuary. It was our favorite Sunday pastime and one that Mother may not have fully endorsed but did not curtail. She might even have welcomed the opportunity to take us there early so that we could expend some of our energy before the other parishioners arrived and the regular service commenced. As far as we were concerned, once the preacher took over the pulpit, the fun ended and the ordeal began.

Church services in those days were neither as sophisticated nor predictable as they are today. The preacher had carte blanche to keep us for as long as he felt so moved by the Spirit. According to Mama, we could thank our lucky stars we were Baptists and not "holy rollers," as she referred to Pentecostal devotees. Mama said holy rollers yelled and screamed and rolled around on the floor during the sermon, and that sometimes their morning church service ran right into the night service. The only noises made at our church during the preacher's sermon were the agreeing "Amens," periodically interjected by one of the men, and an occasional heartfelt "Hallelujah" exhaled by a Spirit-filled congregant. Our preacher was loud and long-winded aplenty for me, especially when he got going on one of his breathless, repetitive torrents. The blood rushed to his face, and he talked so fast there was no time for him to catch his breath as he laid at the congregation's feet the litany of sins we had one and all committed. From the tender age of three, my sinful nature was firmly established in my psyche.

Papa was a preacher, too, and he and Mama had donated the land on which the Carey Springs Missionary Baptist Church and the associated cemetery were built. By the time I heard Papa preach, he was no longer a hellfire and damnation preacher, but his tenets still required a life of vigilant renouncement of earthly pleasures. Along the way, Papa had become an itinerant minister, giving up the role as pastor of the local church to answer his calling to lead revival meetings and Sunday services throughout Pontotoc and Calhoun Counties. It is not for me to question whether it was God's call for Papa to pursue an alternate way of serving Him or a refusal to compromise that propelled Papa to become a circuit riding preacher. What I do know is the call came about the time he refused to allow the daughter of a close neighbor and member of the congregation to attend services until she renounced dancing as a sin of the flesh and ceased the ungodly activity. The abomination the young girl committed was not dancing half-naked around a pole, as might be the modern-day version of the transgression. In those days, dancing was just dancing. Judging from the reaction of the girl's father, Papa must have used strong language to demonstrate the unchristian nature of the girl's behavior. He took sufficient umbrage at Papa's portrayal of his daughter's sinful behavior that he insisted our grandfather issue an apology from the pulpit. When Papa refused to alter his position, the girl's father got so fired up he waited for Papa in front of the church at the conclusion of the service, carrying a large knife he planned to use on our grandfather. One of the other parishioners got wind of the plan, and several of the men slipped Papa out the side door.

It is difficult to reconcile this aspect of Papa's personality with the loving grandfather who bounced Betty, Tony, and Cindy on his knee as he made up songs christening Tony as Toni and Cindy as Cindi. Impossible to square is the godly man who gave so much not just to his family but also sacrificed to help others in need with the stoic man who placed each baby kitten born to Mama's old cat into a tow sack, walked purposefully to Fulton's Pond, and dropped the sack and its contents into the muddy water. Mother explained these behaviors by reminding us that times were financially difficult, that there were already too many mouths to feed, and that it was kinder to kill a kitten than to send it away to wander in search of food and eventually starve to death. I soon stopped going out to the crib to play with the new litters, feeling no need to get attached to animals that were here today and gone tomorrow. Also, I could not ignore the similarities between the kittens and my siblings and I.

What is apparent is that the man who had a heart of gold was supported by a spine of steel. As much as I loved and respected Papa, there was no way to identify someone whose religious and moral convictions were as strong as his. As a traveling minister, Papa was gone for weeks at a time, and Mama's role in the family changed dramatically. Mother recalls the family traveling long distances in a wagon to attend Papa's revival services, and riding back home on dark, bumpy roads that shook the floor boards she, her sister Louella, and her brother Lowell lay upon too much for them to sleep, even when buffered by the quilts Mama spread out for them. By the time I knew her, Mama rarely attended church, though her Christian faith remained rock solid. How a minister's wife escaped the requirement for regular church attendance is baffling. But then, being a preacher's wife was not part of the bargain when she married at the age of fifteen, and it came as a hard blow when Papa got the calling after they had produced three offspring. Mama did not shed tears about much of anything, but she reportedly cried for three weeks when Papa told her the news. When her grieving period ended, in keeping with her strong and responsible nature, she pulled herself together and took on an extra load at home to allow Papa to fulfill his responsibilities. After working with Papa and their three children in the fields, she would scrub Papa's shirts with Lye soap on a scrub board until they were as white as snow. Then she starched the shirts with cornstarch, sprinkled them with water from a soda bottle capped with a tin stopper punctured with holes, and ironed them until they could almost stand independently. She made sure our grandfather looked the part of the man he was—one to be treated with respect.

It was not just Mama's irregular church attendance that was a departure from the role of a preacher's wife. She was known to drop an indelicate word here and there, to which Papa would say, "Now, Lula Mae." His strongest expression of dismay was an occasional "Pshaw," which never seemed to carry the appropriate punch. For instance, Mama demonstrated the absurdity of impotent actions by likening them to "fartin' in a whirlwind," and she let the forbidden word "shit" slip when sufficiently agitated. Local folks did not seem to think less of Mama for not being seated in church on a regular basis or for her directness. Probably that was because she was a good neighbor, ready to do her share and more in their time of need. Sometimes Dena and I walked with her to a neighbor's house one or two miles away to take some of her prized tomatoes or a mess of beans, or to take a prepared dish if one of them was sick.

Our favorite excursion with Mama was to see Miss Emma (pronounced Emmer) Miller, a woman who was far removed from civilization not just in location but lifestyle. She dressed exclusively in black including the bonnet, rode everywhere in a horse-drawn wagon driven by Mr. Wise, her husband—though neither the last names nor the prefix acknowledged that marital status—and was our first introduction to supreme eccentricity. She was not, however, the first eccentric person with whom our family was acquainted. Certainly, our cousin, George Marion, who ordered dresses from Sears and Roebuck in anticipation of receiving the women who modeled them and built a house without windows so that people could not look inside, fit that description. He was more than just "curious," (pronounced keerse) though he was described in this kinder way since he was a relative.

Miss Emma had an even greener thumb than Mama, a trait Mama admired, and whereas we usually delivered cuttings to other folks, we always came home from Miss Emma Miller's house with flowers to plant. Dena and I were sure Miss Emma was a witch, looking as she did so much the part and confirmed by her high-pitched tone reminiscent of the Wicked Witch of the West from the *Wizard of Oz*. She was probably Mama's best friend, though on the surface that was as unlikely a pairing as one could fathom. Maybe they recognized in each other a common independence and a determination to be true to their own natures rather than society's definition of what befit their roles.

In our area, with the exception of the annual sacred harp singing each Father's Day at the Carey Springs Missionary Baptist Church, revivals were the social events of the summer season. Harp singing lasted only one day, and children were not required to attend. However, the proximity of the church to Mama and Papa's house assured that we heard the chanting of the notes, followed by the words, loud and clear from ten in the morning until late afternoon. In spite of how strange harp singing sounded at the time, it likely strengthened my attraction to the sacred Native American chants that Papa unwittingly introduced to us. Revivals lasted most of a week and were viewed as an opportunity for the membership of the hosting church to be renewed, with their commitments to God and the church strengthened and unsaved souls won over to Christ, snatched from the devil's grasp. These annual events were both welcomed and dreaded. During the week the Randolph Baptist Church was in revival, students at the Randolph School were dismissed to attend the mid-morning services. I do not recall any Catholic, Methodist, or Jewish, if there were any, protestations surrounding the preference shown to the Baptist denomination. Students saw it as a reprieve from classes, as we marched like good Christian soldiers half a mile down the gravel-covered Topsy Road to the red brick church around ten o'clock in the morning and back again just in time for our lunch break.

It was the altar call at the end of the service that gave me pause. These invitations to repent of our sins and be saved, walking down the aisle to make a public profession of our faith, started out with a gentle tone at the beginning of the week. The fervor increased by mid-week to a strong beacon and, by week's end, became a command performance. At a late-week service when I was nine years old, the look on the preacher's face the fourth time through the last stanza of "Just as I Am" was distraught, so certain was he that someone was refusing to heed God's call. He looked right at me, more likely than not because of the stricken expression on my face, and before I knew it, I was halfway down the aisle facing a smiling pied piper. The church members all came up to shake my hand after the service, congratulating me on my decision. I was so stricken by what I had done that I just wanted to throw up. When my classmates returned to school, I had to stay behind so the revival preacher could counsel with me about the decision I had made to follow Christ and about the need to be baptized along with the other converts at Fulton's Pond the following Sunday. This, he said, was my opportunity to follow Christ's example by being buried with him, and to arise a new person, washed clean of my sins.

Mother was not attending church during my confessional period, occurring as it did during her five-year hiatus from leaving our yard, a self-imposed confinement that began when Daddy took his leave. That night, when I finally summoned the courage to tell Mother what I had done, she suggested I might not have heard the call as clearly as

I imagined and suggested I wait to see if I received a more distinct summons before being baptized. In the Baptist faith, baptism is almost as important as conversion, and you do not want to do it twice. It is for life, since once saved and baptized, you are permanently out of Satan's reach. That is not to say you might not commit a sin, but after you are saved, the old boy cannot claim your soul. On the other hand, a dunk in the pond without the conversion experience is just a swim and could be perceived as mockery of God. So I happily took Mother up on delaying the underwater excursion. Even in her diminished state, Mother was prescient. Several years later, during Bible study in the classroom of the school's meanest teacher, I heard Jesus calling, really heard him calling, and it was as sweet as the sound of my mother's voice calling us home for supper.

My favorite visits to church were the annual gatherings to celebrate the lives of our deceased loved ones, an event referred to as Memorial Day. Each year on the first Sunday in August, the graves in the Carey Springs Cemetery were decorated with brightly colored plastic flowers. After the flower arrangements were placed on the headstones, we gathered in the church for a special service. On Memorial Day, the focus of the sermon was the promise of a reunion in heaven with those we had lost. It was the most upbeat refrain of the year, full of hope for those who believed that Jesus was the son of God sent to save the world. The one caveat the preacher inserted was the inability for those who did not believe in Jesus to be reconnected with the faithful after death. The service concluded with hymns that spoke of reunion with the dead, such as "When We All Get to Heaven," or "Will the Circle be Unbroken." Memorial Day was not the time for promoting angst but rather for celebrating the lives of the deceased. The images of the reunion conjured up when hearing these songs were unlike the horrible ones that came to my mind when contemplating the rapture prophesied to occur just before Armageddon. The preacher said believers would be called from their graves to give account of their lives and then go straight to heaven or hell. I pictured skeletons rising from the graves and walking around the cemetery as they awaited a detailed review of their lives followed by sentencing. There would be no opportunity for appeal.

The best part of the day was the meal we enjoyed after the sermon ended. Each woman prepared her best dishes, and they were all placed on two long tables constructed under the trees. This veritable feast was referred to as "dinner on the ground," probably because we sat any place we could find to enjoy the food, and that was often on the ground. When I lived in Mexico years later, I discovered that they celebrate their dead in a similar way in what is termed the Day of the Dead, except they dine on the graves of the departed.

In the religion of my youth, the most important day of your life was not the day you married or the day you had a child. It was the day you were saved. That was the day your name was recorded in the Lamb's Book of Life, ensuring you would live forever in heaven, walking streets of gold, and would avoid being sent to hell to burn for an eternity. Prayers for loved ones focused not so much on their worldly success as on their relationship with God and their preparedness for death. Though the lesson of the redeemed thief crucified at Jesus' side confirmed that a deathbed conversion was as effective in ensuring safe passage into heaven as a lifetime of commitment to the Lord, it was risky to wait since you might die quickly and not get another chance to accept the call, or Jesus might grow weary of pursuing you and harden your heart so that your spirit could not hear the next one. My conversion was the best thing that had happened to me in life, as it gave me someone on whom I could rely for love and acceptance. At last, here was a male figurehead who would not desert me. My heart overflowed with praise, and the poems of love for the creator flowed with ease from my pen.

It may have been the depth of my spiritual conviction that sent me over the brink at age sixteen when I first encountered my sexuality. Or it could have been delayed trauma from my near-death experience the previous spring. Admittedly, I had glimpsed my dark shadow on multiple occasions, like when at age seven I terrorized Dena, a foot taller than me, by pushing her in a ditch because she would not stop taunting me. Or when I hid the fact that when hoeing the garden, I had mistaken Mother's young okra plants for weeds, and after cutting all the plants down, stood them back up hoping my error would go undetected. Or the time at age twelve when I had kissed Bobby Ferguson on the return bus trip from the Shiloh National Military Park, a Civil War battleground. Still I was unprepared for the guilt that flooded my being when, at age sixteen, I became sexually aroused. I did not have sex, no matter how Bill Clinton defined it, but the desire was so intense I was convinced of my moral depravity.

Torture best describes the agony I experienced that summer, as Jesus turned his face from me just months after leading me safely around the River Styx. I read the Bible voraciously, looking for some phrase that would assure me I would not perish for my sins and that Jesus would turn his face toward me again. The internal struggle worsened steadily, producing nightly visions of the beasts of Armageddon riding over the hill, riding fast and spitting fire as they pursued me. Sleep offered no reprieve as the demons found their way into my dreams. I pleaded with Jesus to tell me why he had left me, but he was gone from me and only a void remained. Desperate, I went to see Brother Jones, the minister leading our revival that year, pleading with him to tell me how to find Jesus again. He confirmed my fear that the lust in my heart had caused Jesus to turn from me, and he said my only hope was to renounce my sinful nature. I left the preacher that day feeling doomed, knowing that my body would again and again betray my best intentions.

Even as I cried day and night and my family worried that I was having a nervous breakdown, there was no discussion of seeking the help of a mental health professional. There *were* no mental health professionals in our area. We rarely went to a doctor when we were physically ill, so a mental health provider could hardly have been contemplated. In our world, if a person became incapable of coping mentally, she was sent to the state mental hospital at Whitfield, usually without a return ticket. It was more or less assumed that if you got right with God and pulled yourself up by your bootstraps, any psychological problem would resolve itself. A few years earlier, Papa had fallen off a truck bed while helping to unload its contents and landed on his head, producing a breakdown of sorts. He was sent to a "special" unit at Gartley-Ramsey Hospital in Memphis, but that topic was not openly discussed.

After years of searching, prayer, and introspection, I did find God again—in my son's face and in the faces of the other people I love, in the eyes of the down and out and the victorious, the first hyacinth in spring, a snow-covered landscape, a morning sunrise, and on a mountaintop in Peru. In time, God turned his face toward me again, a kinder more forgiving face than the one I remembered. I have learned that severe depression and other forms of mental despair can cause us to feel that we are alone, separated even from God. I have come to believe that God does not hide his face when we need him most, but that great faith is needed to sustain us when we cannot see or feel God's presence. If the darkness lasts too long, even the strongest faith may not be enough to help a person hold on until the light returns.

That dark night of the soul during my sixteenth year heralded my first encounter with depression. This is the same malady that caused our mother to confine herself to our home and yard for several years, unable to allow affection to penetrate the barrier it created, either going out or coming in—the same illness that propelled Dena to attempt suicide as a young woman. When depression strikes, I am never sure whether it is the illness or my soul that convinces me God has deserted me. Who can say where the mental and the spiritual overlap? I do know it sometimes takes all the faith I can muster to survive the darkness. Even when medical professionals tell me it is my brain that is unwell, it feels like a sickness of the soul, a punishment visited upon me for my shortcomings. It helps to believe that sin does not cause God to leave me, that it is the illness that fabricates that delusion.

Faith in God is one of the greatest gift our grandparents and our mother gave my siblings and me. Without that faith, we would not have survived many of life's hardships. Faith is the bedrock of hope, and hope can get a person through many difficulties. Faith and hope are the treasures that old-time religion bestowed upon us. But early exposure to a strident religion is also a curse, perpetuating the belief that the human nature with which we are endowed represents a sinful state. Just as in Biblical accounts, those with mental afflictions were thought to be possessed by demons, the religion of my youth taught me that my mental distress was caused by my own depravity and my failure to resist Satan's temptations.

A familiar hymn proclaims about the old-time religion, "It was good for Hebrew Children and it's good enough for me …." The old-time religion was good enough for my ancestors, too, but I for one am thankful that religious doctrines have evolved along with other aspects of our Southern culture. That old-time religion was much too good for someone as human as me.

SAMSONITE SOJOURNS

For two otherwise savvy people, my brother James and his wife Marie were exceedingly slow in identifying the link between the high school graduation presents bestowed upon their siblings and the revolving door to their home. For each of our graduations, they presented us with a three-piece set of luggage. Quite soon thereafter, we deposited our colorful large bags and matching overnight cases on their guest room floor. Dena and I invaded their residence, me with my blue set and Dena with her coral bags, the same year Marie's sister, Sandra, moved out with her green ones. After our move in with them, luggage went out of vogue as Marie and James' present of choice. That explains why, ten years later, BJ's belongings were ferried to Dennis' and my Birmingham home in a Rubbermaid clothesbasket and why Tony arrived ten years after that lugging his possessions in an Air-Force-issued duffel bag. Our baby sister, Cindy, broke the trend of younger siblings moving in with the older ones to get a start on life, or in some cases, a restart. She did, however, move in with husbands - several. I guess everyone needs somewhere to put their bags when they leave the nest.

In fairness, you could say Cindy initiated at an early age the trend of using graduation luggage for adventurous wanderings from home. When she was eight, she concealed Dena's overnight bag under her coat and took it to school. The protrusion beneath her coat was obvious, but when asked about it, Cindy informed us she was returning a number of books to the school's library. That afternoon, she happily boarded the No. 13 school bus for an unapproved weekend getaway to her friend Jennifer Tutor's house. As the oldest child living at home at that time, looking after the house and my younger siblings were my responsibilities. Consequently, when Cindy did not return from school, I was beside myself. BJ, Tony and I walked miles through a cold rain that afternoon in search of our missing sister. Only the keen eye of our principal, Mr. Hood, who had seen Cindy board the bus with Jennifer, allowed us to track her down that night. When Mother came home from work, Mr. Hood drove her to the Tutor household, several miles away. They came back with a perplexed Cindy in tow, apparently bewildered that we had noticed her absence.

Prior to arriving in James and Marie's spare bedroom, my blue bags had a sojourn to Daytona Beach for our class's senior trip. From ninth through twelfth grades, each

Randolph High School class earned money by picking cotton one or two days each fall and sponsoring cake walks in order to cover the cost of a class trip at the conclusion of senior year. Our excursion was to Daytona Beach, Florida. Due to an innocent incident on that vacation, my best friend, Glenda Houpt, and I became persons of interest to the FBI

Our chariot to Daytona was a yellow school bus identified by large black letters as Property of Pontotoc County Schools, Bus No. 21. During our stay, two young but renowned bank robbers from Pontotoc spotted the bus parked in front of the Thunderbird Lodge. Having been on the lam for a while and lonely for home, they came strolling into the lobby to scout out a familiar face. Several members of our female contingent were hanging out there. It is not clear who was more lacking in good judgment, the two men or Glenda and me, as we readily joined in when the good-looking fellows who said they were from our home county struck up a conversation. Although the alleged felons' photos were among other pictures in area post offices denoting their status as wanted fugitives, mug shots that Glenda and I perused routinely when we skipped study hall so that I could make my daily trek to the post office in search of the money Daddy didn't send, neither

Glenda nor I recognized them. As luck would have it, two of our classmates recognized the cute guys. After our compatriots enlightened us about them, we reluctantly sent the bandits on their way. Still, as a tribute to the bank robbers' cuteness and charm, we all made a pact not to report the desperados to the authorities. We rationalized that it could be a case of mistaken identity, and any intervention on our parts might lead the police on a wild goose chase.

Within twelve hours of arriving back in Randolph, two men in a long black car pulled off the blacktop in front of our house and parked the car. The men, dressed in matching black suits, stepped out of the automobile and walked up to the front porch where Dena and I sat rocking while I filled her in on every aspect of the trip. They summoned me to the back seat of the car for an inquisition, complete with photo recognition. It seems one of our friends could not refrain from telling her mother about her brief encounter with outlaws, and her mother called the sheriff, who contacted the FBI. About a week after the initial discussion with authorities, Glenda and I were abducted from a street in downtown Pontotoc and escorted to the same black sedan for further inquiry. It was sufficiently intimidating and disgraceful to be picked up by the authorities that we quickly spilled our guts. We never knew if our reluctantly provided information assisted in the seizure of the courteous fugitives, but they were apprehended within weeks. Already my newly acquired Samsonite was taking me in new directions.

Larry was the first of us to move in with James and Marie. I suspect James and Marie would agree that Larry added more humor to their lives than any other sibling. Deaf from age two-and-a-half as the result of spinal meningitis, his other senses kicked into overdrive, especially those that attract the opposite sex. Actually, that was a gift Tony shared, leading one to conclude that not only do women love outlaws like babies love stray dogs, but also that women cannot get enough of the dark, silent type. Larry's gift has also been his curse, having spent much of his lifetime escaping the clutches of one female or another. In his early twenties during his first stay with James and Marie, he had not perfected a technique for separating gently from his love interests when the bloom was off the rose. While he was staying at James's, a particularly difficult breakup was at hand. Possessing a soft heart, Larry was in a quandary about how to pull the plug on the relationship without causing the spurned girlfriend too much pain. Then he stumbled upon a solution.

One Sunday, in the early morning hours, a phone call from a tearful young woman jarred James and Marie from sleep. They became wide awake when Larry's girlfriend asked them to share the details of Larry's death. A friend of his had called to inform her of the tragedy but had provided no specifics. After James's heart resumed beating, he hung up and called the morgue. When he was told that no one fitting Larry's description was there, he called the emergency rooms of every hospital in the Memphis area. About an hour later, Larry came strolling through their back door, sporting his usual lighthearted smile, and upon seeing their distraught faces, signed and shrugged, "What?"

Seeing that Larry was not dead, James expressed his outrage as he related the girl's story and asked where she had gotten the idea Larry was dead. Larry found this rather humorous, pleased as he was with the coup he had pulled off. He said he had been ready to break up with the girl, but she was so much in love with him, he had not been sure she could handle the rejection. That was when he came upon a solution that would let her down easily: he would just let her think he had died. As far as I know, that was the closest any of our brothers and sisters ever came to leaving James's house in a body bag.

Dena also put some mileage on her graduation luggage before depositing the bags in James and Marie's house. Soon after Dena's high school graduation, she packed all her clothes into her three-piece set of coral luggage for her planned marriage to the cousin of our across-the-road neighbor, a good catch from a well-respected family in Batesville. Our neighbor was not at all well-to-do, but her sister had married above their family's social standing. Knowing we did not have a proverbial pot to pee in and wanting their son to be married in a manner befitting his social status, the groom's family planned the wedding at their own expense. The night before the wedding day, everything was ready... everything that is except Dena. Just hours before the nuptials were to take place, she realized she did not love the would-be groom, and immediately called off the wedding. Emotions ran high, so Dena packed her luggage and requested that her jilted fiancée drive her home. The route to Randolph passed by Sardis Dam, and for a while Dena feared she might be thrown into the waters below. Thinking strategically, she announced a change of heart in the question of marriage, which lasted just long enough to ensure her a safe passage home.

Dena's coral bags and my blue ones held all our worldly possessions when we moved to James and Marie's house sometime later. Not long after the embers from Dena' cigarette burned a gaping hole in Marie's new sofa, our bags transported our finery into a midtown guesthouse apartment. Several years later, Dena's luggage accompanied her and her son Kevin through several moves from one midtown Memphis apartment to another. Mine got their share of wear and tear touring the United States and as many countries as possible. By the time they were discarded, the locks no longer worked and the sides sagged from having been sat on too many times in order to latch the clasps.

Years later, Tony's extended visits with James and Marie coincided with run-ins with the legal system for drug-related infractions and his need to find a safe house. It was probably not just his affinity for James that drew him to their home. It did not hurt that Marie worked as a business manager for a physicians' practice, which Tony saw as an avenue to prescription drugs. Marie withstood his badgering, and he failed in his attempts to solicit medication.

Tony may not have possessed a three-piece set of matching luggage, but he did carry some baggage. By the time he came to live with Dennis, our son Ryan and me, he was twenty-nine and had just been released from jail after serving six weeks for attempting to sell drugs to an undercover agent. An addict from age fifteen, Tony had supported his habit by working on a riverboat that took him up and down the Mississippi River for two-to-three months at a time. While on the boat, he managed to stay clean, but as soon as he stepped onto the dock in Memphis, he cashed his check, paid his child support, bought his daughter Heather some clothes and then proceeded to shoot every remaining dollar into the hole in his veins and soul.

On what would turn out to be his last shore leave, Tony's funds were depleted before it was time to get back on the boat, and needing money to buy heroin, he resorted to selling drugs. His customer turned out to be a drug enforcement agent. That transaction was actually the best thing that ever happened to Tony because while out on bail from the Tupelo County Jail, he spent a month in a drug rehab unit of the North Mississippi Medical Center and achieved a state of sobriety he was able to maintain.

Just out of rehab when he arrived at our house, duffel bag in tow, Tony still had a few rather major obstacles to overcome. His arrest brought not only a felony charge but also allowed other municipalities to pursue him for several longstanding traffic violations. He was broke with no likely possibility of employment, devoid of a vehicle or a driver's license, and was facing some serious jail time. After a lot of anguished soul searching, he agreed to turn state's evidence against one of the largest drug dealers in North Mississippi, wearing a wire in order to achieve the authorities' desired goal of arresting the drug kingpin. From that point on, he was the target of several disgruntled individuals who were arrested as part of the bust, and because he was our houseguest, we were vulnerable by association.

The luck of the Irish and his guardian angel kept Tony safe, and between my taxi service transporting him to and from Narcotics Anonymous (NA) meetings several nights a week and Dennis apprenticing him in the carpenter's trade, he not only stayed clean but acquired a skill he could use without undergoing a background search. He assisted Dennis in building a house that summer, and soon thereafter found a job as the handyman, carpenter, and landscaper for an affluent and benevolent Birmingham family. On the side, he became an auto dealer, buying clunkers at auctions that he restored to good running condition before selling them. With help from family and friends, he pulled himself out of the hole he had dug, bought ten acres of land about twenty miles north of Birmingham, and became a respectable, if somewhat eccentric, landowner. In addition to the challenges Tony had to overcome, he also had a lot of amends to make to those he had harmed. The things we put into our bags have a way of showing up years after we acquire new ones.

My Samsonite bags have been replaced many times, as I seem to have a fetish for acquiring containers that I can refill and a gypsy spirit that propels me to travel. Through all our journeys, James and Marie have remained a family mainstay, and along with Mother, keep us rooted and connected, ensuring that our sojourns include at least one each year back home to be with the family. It seems James and Marie gave us not just luggage for our travels but additional roots that keep us connected to our Mississippi home.

TAMMY WYNETTE: A SISTER OF SOUL?

Several years ago, a newspaper article announcing Tammy Wynette's death mentioned her strong connection to the working-class man and woman. Her death started me thinking about a time when the lyrics she sang touched a personal chord in me, and it occurred to me that her music was another form of soul music, though not the kind we think of as part of that genre. Her version of soul appeals primarily to rural, white, blue-collar workers, a kind of *country* soul.

For one unforgettable summer during the mid-sixties, I worked at a pants factory in a small town north of the Delta, the same plant where Dena was employed. True to Mrs. Pickens', the literature teacher at Randolph High School, favorite quote from Robert Browning that "a man's reach should exceed his grasp, or what's a heaven for?" , I considered myself a short-timer in the sewing arena, planning to work just long enough to earn enough money to cover my first year's tuition at Itawamba Junior College. I knew nothing about the existence of scholarships or grants, and even though I made A's throughout high school, my teachers did not alert me to those possibilities.

My brief employment at the pants factory turned out to be life-altering, teaching me not only to fully appreciate each subsequent job but to ponder many times the lives of those people whose existence is drowned out by the steady hum of machines, punctuated periodically by shrill bells that signal smoking and lunch breaks. A manufacturing plant has a rhythm unlike that of other workplaces, with the noise from machines taking precedence over the sound of voices or computer keyboard clicks, with each day a mirror image of the one before. Our workday moved into gear at six fifteen a.m., when the sound of a car horn signaled that our carpool had arrived. The driver gathered five workers from within a ten-mile range and deposited us at a factory twenty miles south in time to punch the time clock at seven. In return for her troubles, on payday, she received five dollars from each rider. Our arrivals and departures coincided with numerous carpoolers, since most of the plant's employees commuted a similar distance.

The instant our time cards were punched, we scurried wordlessly to our work stations. If we were to make production, we could not dawdle. "Production" was the minimum output a worker was required to achieve and maintain in order to keep her job. At the pants factory, employees were given three months to make production or be canned. Production was set at 1,057 pairs of pants per day, a number achievable only by working full steam all day. Workers received piecework payment for any pants completed beyond that threshold, but since management raised the production level whenever most of the workers exceeded it, those incentive payments were small. On the day that a new worker met her quota for the first time, the line supervisor rewarded her with a necklace fashioned from string with a button as the gemstone, and that piece of threaded jewelry was proudly worn around the recipient's neck for the remainder of the day.

I was part of the Sewing Department's crew. The pants arrived in our area after workers in the Cutting Department had carefully fashioned them into pattern pieces. Each person in our unit had a specific task to complete before passing the pants off to the next worker, and mine was the ticket-tacking and cuffing functions. I tacked the ticket on at the waistline, turned up the cuffs one inch, and inserted a small set of stitches to secure the cuffs in place. This was one of the easiest jobs in the plant, reserved for rookies like me. For example, Dena attached the belt loops, one of the more time-consuming aspects of assembling a pair of trousers, and Ella Jean, the woman adjacent to me, inserted the pockets into the pants, an exacting process that required skill. Whether they were paid a higher rate to reflect the difficulty of their task, I never thought to ask. Because my task was relatively easy, I made production in just three weeks.

My perspective regarding assembly-line work was that it was sufficiently dehumanizing to be given mindless tasks for eight hours a day and unforgivable that management found ways to further diminish our human dignity. For example, workers could go to the bathroom only with permission from the line supervisor, and should you linger too long, she would appear outside your stall to check on your progress. We were given a seven-minute break in the morning and afternoon, initiated and concluded by a bell. As a newcomer, I had just opened a pack of nabs, as peanut butter and cracker snacks were called, and taken a drink from a bottle of a Pepsi-Cola when the bell ended my first break. I quickly learned to keep coins for the vending machines ready and to swallow bites before they were chewed. Since then, I have not been able to stop swallowing my food while it is still whole.

The lunch bell rang at noon, and at one minute past, a swarm of bodies filled the parking lot, rushing to scarf down the sandwiches they had tucked inside brown paper sacks early that morning. Eating quickly allowed us to salvage a few minutes of our break to cruise downtown before the bell rang at twelve thirty. Eating out was reserved for paydays, partially because of time constraints but, more important, to save money. Payday came every Friday, and had the management suggested a movement to biweekly payrolls, a revolt would have ensued. Getting by from week to week was challenging enough, and fourteen days between paychecks would have been unthinkable. Monday through Thursday, at twelve fifteen, 90 percent of the cars in the factory's lot cranked up and formed a procession around the center of town, returning at twelve twenty-five, just in time for the occupants to punch the clock and be back at their work stations when the bell rang. Fridays were payday, and consequently, had a different pattern associated with them. On those days, we rushed to the bank to cash our paychecks, pulled into a burger joint for a burger, fries, and sweet tea, and rushed back to the plant.

I thought my distinction as valedictorian of my graduating class meant the world was my oyster waiting to be pried open to reveal the pearl designed specifically for me. Now I know that what it really meant was that I was a novice in the lessons of life, not yet sufficiently acquainted with the humility one gains from longing for an elusive goal. I wanted a career, and tacking tickets on pants was a job. This difference in the two was obvious in the conversations among coworkers. The one thing we did not do as we cruised was talk about our jobs. Oh sure, we would occasionally curse our line supervisor or speculate about how many men Pauline, the sexy woman in the Shipping Department whose cleavage was so prominently displayed, had slept with in a given month. We talked about the cute new guy in the Cutting Department and wondered if he was engaged. But we never talked about our work. Maybe this early training explains why it disturbed me later in life when co-workers insisted on talking shop during lunch. Invariably in white-collar jobs, someone wants to talk about work-related problems or cutting-edge ideas. For instance, later in life, when I was a financial officer, one of my controller's favorite lunchtime topics was the most recently issued statement from the Financial Accounting Standards Board, the body that governs how the industry accounts for and reports various financial transactions. Not the most inspirational lunchtime conversation.

As a line worker, what was there to say? I might have said to Ella Jean, "Gosh, Ella Jean, tell me about the technique you use to put those pockets in so smoothly," and she might have replied, "I have made this revolutionary discovery that could change the future of pocket insertions." But we did not say those things, and for obvious reasons. Our jobs took all our physical reserves yet tapped less than a millionth of our brains' capacity.

We did not trouble ourselves about whether the pants production industry became more profitable or more efficient. We did not care because the owners did not care about our opinions or about us. The workers were necessary attachments to the company's machines. If the processes were further automated, the level required for production would be raised but not the wages. Nor would the workers be treated with more respect or asked for suggestions for making their jobs more rewarding. The worker would not receive more time off, since no matter how long you worked for the pants factory or how productive you were, you were given one week's vacation annually when the plant closed for the week of July Fourth. Most of the folks who worked there knew they would be clocking in at seven a.m. and cutting or stitching trousers until they could collect Social Security or until they slumped at their machines for their final break.

It was with our machines that my co-workers and I silently communicated. We spoke to them of our dreams and our fears. The company bought our bodies at a bargain price for eight hours a day, but our minds were free to wander where they chose. I suspect that Geneva, the lady directly behind me, poured into her machine the struggles of raising four children without a husband, hoping for guidance on how she would get them through high school and prepared for lives that were better than the one she was living. Ray might have fantasized about how good it would feel at four thirty when the bell rang and Jim Beam would smooth his ragged edges for a few hours. Pauline probably dreamed of the knight in shining armor she would lure on a permanent basis to take her away from her life of hypnotic exhaustion. She had found Mr. Right so many times only to learn that someone else had found and married him first. Before her divorce, Dena prayed over her machine that her husband Butch would stop cheating on her. And I proclaimed to my machine that it should not get too attached to me because I was going to save enough money by September to start college. I vowed not to become intimately familiar with the silent sounds of disappointment I heard ringing in my ears from those around me.

At seventeen, my vision did not extend beyond the drudgery of my co-workers' jobs. I was blind to the sisterhood and brotherhood that connected them in a common bond or the happiness their friendships brought to their lives. I would be much older before I could appreciate the positive aspects of their jobs, the fact that they were free to think thoughts of their own while their bodies operated on autopilot or the absence of hundreds of competing demands on their time. My naive eyes could not detect the shedding of responsibility that took place at the door everyday at four thirty, to be replaced by a cloak of freedom. It did not occur to my young mind that many of them were happy with their work and content in their lives, or that they had outside interests that filled the void their mindless work created.

I did not go to college that fall or the next or the next. Fate had other plans for my life. Instead, during that summer, my kidney function diminished again, and a trip to the specialist in Memphis revealed that the prolific organ had manufactured more stones and the ureter was again malfunctioning. I spent that August as a patient at Baptist Memorial Hospital in Memphis. My hopes of saving enough money for college went underground. When my sister-in-law, Marie, suggested I apply for a clerical job in Memphis, I did just that, going to work as a claims clerk for an insurance company located in the Sterick Building in downtown Memphis.

After working in the cotton fields, Uncle Lowell's drug store, and the pants factory, my office job was a breeze. I was astonished to learn that workers took thirty minute coffee breaks at ten and three, though they were officially allowed only fifteen, and that we were given a leisurely one-hour lunch break. Spurred by my description of life in the big city and the relatively cushy work atmosphere, Dena joined me just two months later as a guest in James and Marie's house and as a worker at USF&G.

The ensuing twelve years held in store a failed marriage to a young man whose wanderlust propelled us to live in four states in four years, and day jobs combined with night classes. My dream of completing an undergraduate degree was delayed for twelve years, but the wait was not for naught. Those years allowed me to taste the bittersweet life Tammy Wynette's music poignantly portrays. The music of folks who long to make a better life for themselves and their children, but for whom luck seems to have taken a break. She speaks to the hearts of those whose wisdom is rarely sought by others who hold the power over their lives. She tells of the sadness of marriage failed, of dreams shattered. Her music is about people who are defeated yet find the strength to try again, who are betrayed and still find it in their hearts to forgive, and who experience losses so stinging that the hurt moves into the heart and lies there just beneath the surface. Tammy Wynette's songs remind us of a spirit strong enough to survive life's obstacles, of love that hangs on through tragedy, and of hope that lies dormant and appears dead only to be awakened on some spring morning when the Dogwood blooms and the Wisteria blossoms. That is country soul music.

LONNIE WAYNE

Not all stories have happy endings. Not every person's happiness outweighs the pain they endure. That does not mean their stories should not be told. In fact, perhaps their stories deserve to be remembered more than others because it is only in the telling of them that their lives have meaning. Lonnie Wayne's saga falls into this category.

Lonnie Wayne was the oldest son of Marlon Stewart, our community's ne'er-do-well. Marlon was the only man in our community who did not hold a job in a factory, operate the general store, farm, teach, or preach for a living. His source of income remains an unsolved mystery. Marlon's unemployment was not the only attribute that differentiated him from his peers. His refusal to wear shoes even on those rare occasions when snow covered the Mississippi hill country was just one of his eccentricities. The residue that coated his body gave his skin a rusty appearance, confirming suspicions that he had not bathed in recent years. His unique smell, a combination of body odor, auto fluids from tinkering with his car, and smoke from the fireplace that warmed their home, announced his presence before his image appeared. Marlon's disposition was even darker than his skin. My shoulders shivered from a chill in my spine whenever he was in our midst.

Marlon's wife, Iona Jean, was as kind as Marlon was harsh. Folks referred to her as *simple*, the term applied to someone with a diminished intellectual capacity. Iona Jean struggled to navigate life's most basic challenges. Mother often commented that situations she considered minor sent Iona Jean into a tailspin. It was the exception rather than the rule for Iona Jean to put a home-cooked meal on the table. The Stewart family's destitute state did not propel Marlon or Iona Jean to make any serious effort to alter their circumstances. They spent more energy lamenting their impoverished lifestyle than it would have taken to improve it. During the occasional spring when Iona Jean planted seeds in the small plot behind the house, she was lackadaisical in tending the plants, allowing weeds to overtake them. She preserved only a few vegetables, not enough to tide the family over during the winter months. Like almost everyone, the Stewarts slaughtered a hog on the first cold November or December morning. Before freezers became standard, it was common practice for families to have a smokehouse where meats were smoked or salt-cured to preserve them. This allowed us to enjoy fatback, country ham, and hog jowl throughout the winter.

The only things we ate immediately were cracklings made from the skin, fried until it was crunchy, liver, tenderloin, and souse meat, a kind of disgusting pâté. Marlon and Iona Jean feasted on every part of the meat as long as it stayed fresh, and did not preserve anything for the future.

Occasionally, through some stroke of luck or a benevolent gesture, Iona Jean would announce that she had acquired five or ten dollars to spend on groceries. She immediately bounced up the hill to Larry Onsby's store and returned home with a carton of Coca-Colas, a few bags of Planter's peanuts and Golden Flake potato chips, Milky Way or Baby Ruth candy bars, a loaf of bread, and two or three cans of Spam or potted meat. Mother shook her head when commenting on the foolish way Iona Jean spent her money, claiming she could have bought enough food to last a month with the same amount of money. I secretly admired Iona Jean's superior culinary taste.

Iona Jean was as incapable of protecting her personal boundaries as she was of managing a household. While other hardworking people in our part of the world protected their belongings with the same diligence exercised in safeguarding their loved ones, Iona Jean left everything open to the world for anyone's use or abuse. Because of that trait, I learned how to sew on the Singer sewing machine that occupied a corner in the Stewarts' dark, dank kitchen. Mama owned a pedal machine just like Iona Jean's, but it was off limits until we took sewing lessons in our ninth grade home economics class. Even afterward, Mama curtailed my use of the machine after she saw the result of my efforts. Declaring the material I had used on my project too expensive to waste, she salvaged a skirt from the peach colored polished cotton dress I had mangled. So it was that at age twelve, I spent several summer afternoons stitching together on Iona Jean's machine the squares Mama had cut up from fabric remnants for my first quilt top.

Pedal machines required one to maintain a certain rhythm on the metal foot plate. Several times each hour, I lost that pace, broke the thread, and called for Iona Jean to help me rethread the machine. There were several points on the arm of the machine that had to be properly threaded, and that presented a challenge for me. Already, my technical difficulties were manifesting. My errors sometimes created knots in the bobbin, which was threaded through the bottom of the machine. Iona Jean exercised the patience of Job in responding to my requests for assistance. Had she been a little bit more like Mama, she would have sent me packing after my first few mistakes and relegated me to stitching together the quilt top pieces by hand. It was not until I broke the only needle she owned that I was banished from her kitchen. It was probably months before she could afford to replace that needle.

Lonnie Wayne inherited his mother's gentle temperament as well as her simple way of thinking. As a teenager, Lonnie Wayne was a handsome lad, and he and I both thought he bore a slight resemblance to the emerging star Elvis Presley. Consequently, Lonnie Wayne spent a good deal of time gyrating his hips while singing into an invisible microphone. Luckily, he inherited some musical talent from his father, and in time a real guitar replaced the imaginary device. He seemed not to notice that his vocal skills had not followed suit. It is a shame he did not improve in tone concurrently with his increase in volume.

Children with learning disorders are frequently shunned by their more astute classmates, and Lonnie Wayne was no exception. His unkempt appearance further distanced him from the boys his age. Lonnie Wayne was a lonely figure. The only occasions when he was not ostracized by his contemporaries were on summer evenings during his teenage years when several of the young boys from the area gathered on the Stewarts' sagging front porch to jam with Marlon and Lonnie Wayne. He became invisible to them as soon as they left his front yard. I admit sometimes turning a blind eye toward him between eight and three on school days, as well.

When we were not in school, Dena and I frequently played with Lonnie Wayne, both figuratively and literally. We challenged him to basketball games like Around-the-World, when, for a period of time, a hoop was attached above the entrance to Marlon's garage. Things had a way of appearing at the Stewart household and just as quickly disappearing. For example, one afternoon when I was twelve and Lonnie Wayne fourteen, I located him in the pasture behind his house, aiming a newly acquired .22 caliber rifle at Coke bottles perched on the posts that supported a barbed wire fence. Like Iona Jean, Lonnie Wayne could not refuse any request I made of him, so he taught me to shoot the rifle. He generously shared the box of bullets he had discovered along with the weapon. We enjoyed two afternoons of target practice before the rifle disappeared from the premises. When Mother asked me what I had been doing at Lonnie Wayne's those afternoons, I told her we had been shooting. No doubt, she thought I meant baskets or a BB gun because she did not get hysterical.

The other sport Dena and I enjoyed was designed to be played on Lonnie Wayne rather than with him. On days when we were particularly bored, we adopted the personas of Victoria and Monica, imaginary cousins of ours who lived in Memphis. Sometimes we became Annette and Darlene from the Mickey Mouse Club. We prissed over to Lonnie Wayne's and introduced ourselves, putting on the proper airs and demeanors of our characters of the day and relating that Linda and Dena were visiting our families while we visited their home. Lonnie Wayne appeared to bite hook, line, and sinker. He asked us all sorts of questions about what it was like to live in a city, where we went to school, what we did for entertainment, and the like. Once we had validated our intellectual superiority to Lonnie Wayne as well as our talent in acting, we left, joking about his gullibility as we crossed the road back to our house. It never occurred to us that Lonnie Wayne was as bored as we were and played along with us as his own escape from reality. We fell for his act. Clearly, Lonnie Wayne was a better actor than we were.

We generally avoided Lonnie Wayne's dad, but sufficiently overcame our fear of him when our TV was out of service. During those frequent outages, we plopped down on one of the two beds in the Stewarts' living room, which served as their only bedroom, to watch *Monday Night at the Movies*. One evening, we saw *An Affair to Remember*, and I fell madly in love with Cary Grant. When ogling William Holden in *The World of Suzie Wong*, who could remember where they were much less with whom they were watching the movie? We also managed to handle our misgivings about Marlon long enough to enjoy Elvis's debut appearance on the *Ed Sullivan Show*.

Those who lived out in the country spent a considerable amount of time out-of-doors. Not only did most of the work take place outside, so did the warm-weather leisure activities, mostly due to the effort to stay cool before air-conditioning became commonplace. The Stewart family spent even more time outdoors than others. In the summertime, they slept on pallets in the breezeway that separated the two inhabitable rooms of their house from the two that were unused. The first of the uninhabited rooms was filled with all sorts of discarded furniture, tools, and implements, and Marlon kept it locked. The other room was off-limits to everyone.

The Stewarts not only lived outdoors, they lived out loud. We were privy to most of their conversations, especially at night, when the only competition with their voices was the drone of our window fan and the night sounds of crickets and katydids. Marlon's tone of voice was generally angry and Iona Jean's apologetic. When his father was around, Lonnie Wayne's voice held a perpetual twinge of fearfulness. That was understandable since he was invariably the target of Marlon's rage. Lonnie Wayne could not do anything that pleased his father. Marlon shouted at Lonnie Wayne about anything and everything. Sometimes, shouting was not enough to quell Marlon's demons. Those were the times the sounds from the Stewart home were almost unbearable to hear. It was impossible to predict when Marlon's bad humor would escalate into rage, or what precipitated the change from verbal to physical expression of his anger. However, the outcome was predictable: Marlon's release would be imprinted on Lonnie Wayne's body.

The pitch of Marlon's incriminating words signaled worse things to come. Safe in my bed, my stomach formed a knot, anticipating the sounds that inevitably followed. First came the snap of the forcefully swung belt, followed by the thud of the buckle as contact was made with Lonnie Wayne's skin. My body cringed with each lash. Lonnie Wayne's agonizing pleas, non-stop throughout the ordeal, seemed to fuel Marlon's heated emotions. When Marlon was tired or calmed, the punishment would cease. Lonnie Wayne's sobs and Iona Jean's cries continued.

The first few times we heard the abuse, we asked Mother to intercede. She was clearly as horrified as we were. Still, she told us she could not do anything about the situation because we did not have a man in the house. Not having a man in the house set us apart in many ways, and having a greater vulnerability was one of them. This was especially obvious after Bobby and James graduated from high school and went to work in Memphis. Would someone enter our house one night through a window propped open for the breeze to enter, or through the latched screen door that separated us from the outside world with its ominous treats? Impending danger loomed large in our minds, with only our mother as protector. Mother said one of the neighborhood men would do something to stop Marlon's abuse of Lonnie Wayne. In spite of my own trepidations about Marlon, I wanted Mother to intervene to save Lonnie Wayne from his tormentor. Only in retrospect did I understand that she was doing what mothers do—protect their young ones regardless of the consequence to others. Mother did not trust Marlon any more than we did, and she feared acts of revenge targeted toward her children.

As an adult, I try not to judge another's actions or lack thereof, because their intentions cannot be known by others. Still, the reality is that none of our neighbors, including Lonnie Wayne's grandfather who lived near enough to hear the pounding on Lonnie Wayne's flesh, took action to save him. It was the way in those days to let each family manage its own affairs and resolve internal differences. Turning a blind eye was the rule rather than the exception. This was true in situations of sexual as well as physical abuse. A young woman who lived a few miles from us was said to have given birth to a son sired by her father. In her case and Lonnie Wayne's, the authorities were not alerted. The younger sister of a friend of mine was killed in the car her drunken father was driving, and there were no legal repercussions. There were other instances of neglect and abuse in our vicinity that went unaddressed. To be fair, a person would have been hard-pressed to find an agency charged with responsibility for investigating charges of child abuse. Consequently, Lonnie Wayne and other children who suffered from similar abuse found no reprieve from the torture inflicted on them.

The lives we lived in those days were freer, and in many ways, more innocent than the lives of our offspring. But children also had fewer advocates for their safety. Though many fall through them, some safety nets do exist for the Lonnie Waynes of today. Some who lament the rampant child abuse of our times believe it is a new phenomenon. Some blame it on the changes in family structure and the resulting decline in family values. They point to the past as a safer time for our children. But those people did not grow up across the road from Lonnie Wayne.

STAYING WARM

In our house, you were never truly warm from the time the first freeze hit until spring arrived. With only wallpaper to cover the cracks between the planks on the walls and linoleum to block the wind between the floorboards, it was impossible to create a toasty environment. Scorch marks on housecoats and jackets served as reminders of the penalty for standing too close to heaters and fireplaces when warming your backside. Houses in the country were heated for sleeping only when the thermometer dipped to ten degrees. Most night, we stayed fairly warm under the mountain of quilts and blankets Mother heaped on top of us. Being part of a large family was a plus in the winter, allowing us girls to sleep three to a bed on the coldest nights. Poor Tony, the only boy at home for most of his life, did not have anyone on whom to inflict his cold feet.

Certain games helped you forget how cold you were. Wintertime diversions that provided an opportunity to wander further into our fantasy worlds were ideal. My sisters and I entered that world through the lives of our paper dolls. We could not purchase books with the detachable cardboard dolls and a multitude of form-fitting fashions.

Our icons were clipped from the Sears and Roebuck catalog, the most versatile of all publications. This alternate
source of images provided flexibility, allowing us to fabri-
cate infinite identities. One of our female characters could
go from blonde to brunette as she changed fashions,
which may account for my propensity to treat my hair like
an artist's canvas, changing the color to match each season's wardrobe. Granted, the models were flimsy, which is
not a commentary on the superficiality frequently ascribed
to people in that profession. The fact that they were so thin
meant they did not last long. On the other hand, their bodies were more flexible than the cardboard counterparts,
and could be bent at the waist and knees to fit into chairs
made from matchsticks, flattened to lie contentedly on
beds of straw, or crumpled up to ride away in a small toy
car turned convertible. Our girls were forever falling in love
with the male model of the day, depending upon the fickle
fancy of the game's producers. Our female dolls were not
limited to one suitor as store-bought versions were.

Pretending took on a different flavor when I held our
baby sister, Cindy, on my knee and played Myrtle and
Girdle, a game I concocted featuring two gossipy old maids
who spoke in high voices, telling tales on all their neighbors, families, and the world at large. Cindy's fascination

with engaging in this game perplexed me, but she never tired of it. Her sole lament was that I would rarely succumb to her appeals to play Myrtle rather than Girdle. Myrtle was the dominant, knowledgeable character, and Girdle was naïve and a bit of a flake. This game provided my one opportunity to assume the character of the wiser person, since in real life Dena had dibs on that role for life. Only when Cindy was infirm did I relinquish the coveted role of the worldlier Myrtle and assume the character of the naïve protégée. Cindy was granted the dominant role for several weeks after she fell out of the oak tree in the side yard while attempting to hang by her knees. I felt supremely guilty about her injury because this was another pastime I taught her, though obviously not too well.

After Daddy left, we confiscated the deck of Rook cards he and Mother had shared with two of their friends in happier times. Rook was king until we misplaced too many of the cards to complete a suit. The game required a foursome, so some combination of Dena, BJ, Tony, Cindy, and I gathered in the kitchen at our dining table on a regular basis. Prior to its demise, we became proficient at our bastardized version of the game.

Losing the Rook cards was a forgivable infraction. Misplacing a bump jack was not. Bump jacks were the long-running favorite winter sport. Our cold kitchen's linoleum floor, slick from multiple coats of Johnson's liquid wax, provided a perfect surface for our quick hands to glide across as we captured the necessary number of jacks and placed them in the other hand before the ball, tossed in the air to commence the cycle, bounced a second time. Unless, of course, you were playing Around the World, Eggs in a Basket, or Pigs in a Pen. In those games, a second bounce was permitted while the player deposited the jacks into the designated place. The number of jacks to be collected increased from one to ten as the player successfully completed the retrieval. Touching any jack not retrieved, dropping a jack, or picking up the wrong number ended the player's turn. We became adept enough to keep these games in progress through extended variations before a victor emerged.

As in most of the houses in our neighborhood, several hooks had been inserted into our living room ceiling. Those hooks were placed there to support wooden frames that were lowered to chair level when it was time to stitch a new quilt. Although the quilters pieced quilt tops with lovely designs, quilting was not considered an expression of art in those days. Rather it was an essential skill if families were to survive freezing temperatures inside poorly insulated houses. Everyone slept under a bounty of quilts. As the weather grew colder, the number of quilts increased, until the weight was so great, it was difficult to turn over in bed.

Mama, Mother, and several of our neighbors spent a day every winter at each of their houses, stitching a quilt for the hosting family. A square of cotton muslin large enough to cover a bed was attached to the frame. Rolls of cotton were spread over that surface. Before the designated day, the hostess pieced together into a pattern scraps from fabrics previously used to make dresses, pants, or blouses. The patterns of squares, rectangles, or triangles had previously been sewn together to form a decorative top for the quilt. After the patchwork top, cotton, and muslin were sandwiched into the frame, the women pulled their straight-back chairs up to the frame's edge and began to stitch through the three layers. The hostess provided the thread, while each participant brought her own needle and thimble, as well as her unique style of stitching. Within the pattern of the patchwork top was emblazoned the artistry of each seamstress.

Quilting Bees did not include children on the guest list, but they were high on the list of parties for children to crash. When held at our house, this was an event Dena and I competed with each other to attend. The one who feigned sickness first stayed home from school to witness the extravaganza, since, apparently, Mother did not believe both of us could be ill on the same day. It was preferable to receive advance notice of the date of the spectacle, so that one could emit signals of an oncoming cold or stomach-ache a day in advance. The downside of that strategy was if the event was delayed, as happened to Dena one year, Mother was not likely to buy off on the excuse a second time. Typically, I would go to school even if I was at death's door, but I went to any length to earn the right to lie on the linoleum floor beneath the wooden frame, warmed by the heat emitted from the butane heater and held captive by the quilt overhead, and listen to Sarah, Iona Jean, Miz Eula, Miz Flora, and Mama converse on a multitude of subjects. Before the day was over, they had updated each other on the lives of everyone and everything for miles around. Mother's mouth was characteristically tightly zipped, so most of the time we were ignorant about the happenings in the area. The Quilting Bee and our annual krauting sessions with Mama provided the best venues for enlightenment.

Once the quilt was finished, Mama would pronounce which of us girls would have the honor of initiating it that night. Sleeping under a new quilt was a coveted honor, since local legend had it that the man a girl was to marry would reveal himself to her in a dream that night. Judging from our marital histories, it seems that Cindy and I slept under more than our share of new quilts.

Once we reached our teenage years, basketball became the primary winter sport. Our house was down the hill from the gymnasium, so we could walk to the home games. All of the county schools had two basketball teams, boys and girls, and one or both of Randolph's teams consistently contended for the county championship, and some of the better teams made it to the state playoffs. The girls' teams were as competitive as the boys', although the girls' game was less taxing since it was played on half the court. I was on the B team during junior high but gave up basketball after eighth grade, having played for thirty seconds in one game. After that, the appeal of the sport was more social than physical. Every cute boy in Pontotoc County entered our gymnasium at some point each winter, and Dena and I were always there to enjoy the parade. Dena didn't even have to pay to attend, because she was selected to be the person who called the *Commercial Appeal* to report the score after each game.

The social attraction of the sport caused us to be much more popular during the playing season than at other times of the year. The only girl we knew who had her own car was my friend Wanda Luther, and that was a mixed blessing, since her car had seen its better days. Wanda had to commence pumping the brakes a quarter of a mile in advance of stopping the automobile. Girls who had no transportation and with whom Dena and I otherwise had little interaction came flocking to us for invites to sleep over on game nights. Dena, who has always been able to say no to anything that doesn't strike her fancy, allowed only her best friend, Joyce Tutor, to stay over, while I entertained lots of newcomers, in addition to my constant buddy Glenda.

By far the cutest boy to enter the gymnasium door arrived before my basketball viewing days. He was a young singer from Memphis who was invited by an astute school secretary in March 1955 to give a live a performance at Randolph High School. Touted for their recordings of "That's All Right Mama," "Good Rockin' Tonight," "Heartbreaker," and "Milk Cow Boogie Blues," he and his band, the Blue Moon Boys, signed a contract to appear for a charge of seventy-five cents for each adult and fifty cents per child. The show was scheduled twice, since weather caused the first appearance to be cancelled. Even though his appearance at our school was just one year before his legendary appearance on the *Ed Sullivan Show*, this young man apparently did not view himself as a star. At the end of the show, he shot baskets with some of the local boys, including Bobby and James.

On that winter night, I am guessing there was not a single person in the Randolph High School gymnasium who thought about being cold, as Elvis Presley lit a fire that is still burning in the hearts of his fellow Mississippians.

IT'S NOT WHAT YOU SAY, IT'S HOW YOU SAY IT

Our mother is a woman of few words. Her predominant communication style is nonverbal. When we were children, she never told us she loved us, a trademark of her generation, I suppose. We inferred that Mother loved us because of her sacrifices on our behalf and her back-breaking efforts to keep us together and meet our needs for survival. She said, "I love you," by making our favorite cakes on our birthdays and preparing the foods we liked best when we were sick. She did not yell at us when our behaviors warranted discipline. A look or the tone of her voice communicated her intended message more effectively than an epistle laced with superlatives. Her children might wisely have emulated this behavior rather than following our natural tendency to vehemently state our points of view, a characteristic inherited from Mama and our father. Mother's carefully framed and delivered words had the power to alter her children's opinions more readily than a vociferous and well-crafted debate. Army sergeants faced with the challenge of reprogramming the psyches of young recruits could learn a thing or two from our mother.

As a single parent in charge of such a large assem-
blage of potential juvenile delinquents, Mother must have
quickly grasped the necessity of establishing her author-
ity. When our behavior deviated too far afield from her
expectations, Mother would find the perfect moment,
usually at the height of our exaggerated confidence as we
ascended toward full and often misguided self-expression,
to puncture with the precision of a marksman our inflated
self-perceptions. She accomplished this objective with a
frugality of words. The independence we gained with age,
professional accomplishments, and life experience altered
only in format Mother's propensity to occasionally "call us
down."

Mother now writes her words on white notebook
paper and delivers them via the U.S. mail in what we af-
fectionately refer to as Nelliegrams. Her daughters are
the primary recipients of these pieces of correspondence,
either because our behaviors deviate farther afield from
her expectations than those of our brothers, or because
she perceives that males are inherently wiser. Nelliegrams
arrive in legal-sized plain white envelopes, which immediately differentiate them from the cards containing heartfelt
messages Mother thoughtfully sends us on birthdays and
at Christmas. Befitting her skill in the art of war as well

as peace, Mother reserves Nelliegrams for particularly egregious trespasses. As an adult, the trepidation I have felt upon receiving one of those envelopes is laughable. After all, I have gone toe to toe with presidents of major universities, reprimanded and terminated employees, testified before state legislators and a governor's task force, traveled as a consultant in Columbia accompanied by armed guards, and jumped from an airplane. Those experiences pale in comparison to the ominous feeling the infamous envelopes evoke. In a flash, I am ten years old again, and Mother has uncovered yet another of my myriad character flaws.

A technique that makes Mother particularly effective in modifying her daughters' behavior is her focus on one deviant at a time. If she targeted more than one of us simultaneously, we might join forces and challenge her assessment. With only one of us temporarily on the spit, the reaction is more likely to be relief by the others that they are not over the flame. While these written communications have not completely lost sway over us with age, we have found a measure of humor in them. Nowadays, when one of us receives a Nelliegram, she calls the others to let them know they are off the hook for the immediate future. As we discuss the latest transgression, we share a chuckle that Mother still sees us as children. Funnier still is that we respond in kind.

I admit that a disconcerting aspect of Nelliegrams is how prescient they often are. Though sometimes overstated, the critique inevitably holds more than a modicum of truth concerning our behavior, and may even point us toward behavior that could improve our character. The unnerving feature is her insight into our personal lives, even those of us who no longer live in her vicinity and share limited information with her about our trials and tribulations—for her protection as well as our own. Limiting our mother's worry list has long been one of our goals, but that does not diminish her ability to intuit the events transpiring in our worlds.

Perhaps Mother's intuitive skills explain her assumption that we know the things she knows before they are verbally relayed to us. Not all Nelliegrams are intended to enlighten her children about personal transgressions. Some of her letters convey other information. Until James gave Mother a cell phone a few years back, important information was communicated through letters. The graver the news, the briefer the message was. If a relative was hospitalized or died, Mother used the mail service rather than Ma Bell to inform us. Even tragic information was delivered in this manner, usually in an oddly placed sentence at the end of a letter, worded something like this: "I guess you knew Carrie died," as though a press conference had been held to announce our aunt's demise.

The most notorious of all Nelliegrams was delivered to me in 1968. I learned of our father's death in an offhand comment at the end of one of Mother's letters. "By the way," she wrote at the bottom of the second notebook sheet of what for her was an uncommonly newsy communication, "Otis died." From the wording, one might have inferred that the family ferret had keeled over. It took a few readings of the newsbreak for it to sink in that my father was not only dead but had already been buried. I was living in Oregon at the time and did not have a telephone. After recovering from the shock, I used a friend's telephone to call Mother and express my feelings of grief about our father's death and my consternation about her method of notifying me. She was as puzzled by my reaction as I was by hers. "Well I'll swan," she said (swan or swanee in this context being the colloquial equivalent of "swear," which she did not), "I didn't dream it would matter that much to you."

Given that our father had not been a real parent to us, Mother's sentiment might be more understandable than mine. This was especially true considering Dena's and my last encounter with him. Our final sighting of Otis occurred aboard a city bus in Memphis, Tennessee. I was eighteen and had taken a clerical job at USF&G Insurance Company with the goal of saving enough money to enter college. Shortly after I went to work, Dena moved north to join me as an employee of the same firm. On the day of the unplanned reunion with our father, we left the office punctually at four forty-five and walked the few blocks to Main Street to catch a midtown bus that would take us to the guesthouse we rented on Peabody Avenue. We had just settled into our seats near the back of the bus when it stopped to allow passengers to board before turning left onto Linden Avenue. Our father was one of the riders who stepped aboard.

We recognized Otis immediately, even though we had seen him only once since he left home when I was eight and Dena eleven, and for only a few moments on that occasion. We nudged each other, stunned to see our father, particularly on a city bus. In our memory, this proud man had always driven a relatively new automobile and would have eschewed public transportation. He was still proud enough to be dressed in his usual white shirt and dark dress slacks, but the shirt lacked the freshly laundered and starched appearance of earlier times. When he took a seat near the front of the bus, we were conflicted about whether we should make ourselves known to the stranger who was our father. In her caustic way, Dena bet me he would not know us if he looked us directly in the face, and true to my Pollyanna nature, I wagered he would. We agreed to test our opposing hypotheses.

According to our hastily designed plan, I was to go to the front of the bus, ask our father to let me into the window seat beside his aisle seat, and watch his response. In the time it took for me to walk from the back to the front of the bus, I started to tremble. Upon arriving at the row of seats where my father sat, I made a big deal of my request for entry. He looked at me, turned aside into the aisle, and permitted me to enter before returning his gaze to the newspaper he had been reading. It was not a surprise that he was reading, since during his visits home, he had always found written material more interesting than getting to know his children.

In the first few moments after my arrival, Daddy showed no recognition of or interest in me, and I became anxious he would get off the bus without looking at me closely enough to realize I was his daughter. Then it came to me! If I asked the time, he would look at me when he replied. So

I asked. He glanced from his watch to me, pronounced that it was ten minutes past five, and continued reading. That is when I realized that to my father, I was just a young girl on a Memphis city bus. A few stops later, he stood up and pulled the cord, signaling his exit at the corner of Mclean and Peabody, a few blocks from our guesthouse.

Dena and I acted as though this poignant scenario meant nothing to us, and an observer would have assumed we shook it off. In fact, we laughed half-heartedly about how predictable his response was, and then we did not speak of it again for years. I don't know about Dena, but several times before marrying two months later and moving to Oregon, I returned to the corner where our father disembarked, hoping for another encounter with him. We never connected. Eight months later, he was dead. And a week after his death, a Nelliegram brought me the news of his final departure.

My siblings and I use humor as a means of alleviating sadness. In the face of a tragic situation, we invariably find something funny about it. In that vein, we have found in this story a humorous punch line. Each time we learn that Mother has once again neglected to inform us of important information, we respond with a wink, "Oh! By the way, Otis died."

ALIEN BEINGS

At age four or five, I saw an African American person for the first time. This fact is not indicative of North Mississippi's racial diversity in the fifties, but rather of the perimeter of our world, which extended no more than two miles in any direction. Our school was not integrated, and there were no African Americans in our community. The sighting occurred late one afternoon on a visit to Larry Onsby's store to purchase a pack of Lucky Strikes for James. Dena and I saw what we could only surmise were people from another dimension—if not from outer space then certainly from another county. We were at once spellbound and terrified, suspecting we were witnessing something from which we should not make too hasty a retreat, lest we forfeit the ability to fully describe the exotic beings. An equally strong fear of being physically abducted and transported to the place of the aliens' origin held us in its grip. In keeping with our typical behavior, we watched intently as several of the interesting beings exited the bed of the light blue pickup truck in which they had arrived, and then we ran home so fast an observer might have inferred we were being chased by a rabid dog.

Out of breath and too excited to speak clearly, we haltingly told Mother what we had seen, halfway expecting her to chastise us for the wild imaginations that compelled us to make up such stories. Surprisingly, she recognized right away the nature of the alien beings we had seen and explained that they were not foreign creatures but human beings with dark skin. They even had a name. Mother said they were Negroes. She said they were probably one of the Negro families that lived up around Springville, a community about five or six miles north on Highway 9. I lay awake for a long time that night, mesmerized by the idea that people could have such different skin colors than mine and still be human beings.

The adults with whom we interacted in our rural area were focused on providing a living for their families. No time or energy was available for consideration of racial issues. The absence of African Americans in our proximity further removed race as a factor in our lives. Until segregation was introduced, I did not hear the locals discuss minorities. Consequently, my next experience involving people of color did not occur until a couple of years later. Dena and I were on one of those rare trips to Pontotoc to visit Uncle Lowell and Aunt Lynda Merle at their drugstore. Aunt Lynda Merle had treated us to dough burgers (ground beef mixed with flour for filler) cooked on the grill in the diner operated out of the basement beneath their drugstore. The burger was followed by one of Uncle Lowell's chocolate milkshakes made especially for us. For customers, milkshakes at the drugstore counter contained three to five scoops of vanilla ice cream—depending on whether you wanted to pay fifteen, twenty, or twenty-five cents—whole milk, and the flavored syrup of your choice, blended to a smooth consistency by the three blades on the milkshake machine. For us, the recipe was altered to begin with ten scoops of ice cream, accompanied by a guarantee from Uncle Lowell that it would put some flesh on our bones unless the tapeworms that kept us so skinny got to it first. Of course, we did not really have tapeworms, because Mother wormed us on a routine basis with some medicinal brew used by all country folks whose children played in the dirt and ate a few mud pies. Children who roamed freely throughout the countryside remained gaunt even if well fed and wormed by their mothers. Mother augmented our diets with cod liver oil to make up for any nutrients the parasites ingested.

After drinking the gigantic milkshake, we were desperate to find a toilet, and since the drugstore did not have one, Aunt Lynda Merle sent us across the street to use the bathroom in another facility. When we arrived, we found there were two bathrooms, one labeled "Colored" and the other one "White." Dena, who read voraciously, and who by then knew something about discrimination, was indignant and said she would not use the white girls' bathroom. I agreed, since I had always been a proponent of color. After all, had I not been so set on a cake with pink icing for my fourth birthday that Mother had resorted to adding beet juice to the seven-minute icing to create the desired color? It tasted horrible, but the color was perfect. In my opinion, color was preferable to white any day of the week. When Dena led the way into the door marked "Colored," I happily followed. This sufficiently disturbed a white woman who saw us go through that door that she rushed into the restroom, took us by the hands, and escorted us through the bathroom door marked "White." By then I did not really care either way because the shade of the bathroom marked "Colored" was not pink or red or anything memorable, and the one labeled "White" was painted the same color. Later when Dena explained the racial nuance, I could not fathom why we could not all just pee together.

My next racial lesson came under the tutelage of Uncle Lowell. From age nine, I worked at the drugstore every

Saturday. One might mistakenly interpret "worked" as an overstatement, given my age, but that was not the case. In those days, even children earned their keep. In fact, Uncle Lowell offered me the job after he observed my industrious nature and decided I would be a "good worker." Each Saturday morning at seven thirty, I rode to Pontotoc with Mrs. Ray, who worked at Stubbs Department Store. After cleaning the glass display cases, I manned the soda fountain for the next twelve hours and assisted in other operations of the store. Although I helped customers find sundry items, selling tobacco products and serving fountain drinks and ice cream were my primary responsibilities. Oddly, adults found it unsettling to have a little girl assist them in locating items, such as Timex watches, lighters, and ornaments for the home, housed in the glass enclosed display cases, but they were quite comfortable purchasing cigarettes, chewing tobacco, or Prince Albert in a can from one.

My take home pay was three dollars a day, or sometimes three fifty if Uncle Lowell was in a particularly benevolent mood. The cost of my ride to and from Pontotoc was a quarter, and I spent another quarter for a milkshake and a pack of nabs, the name we used for peanut butter and cracker snacks, at lunchtime. I made it a point to visit Kuhn's dime store every week on my lunch break to purchase small toys or trinkets for BJ, Tony, and Cindy, who would be impatiently waiting for my return and their surprises. Those little bare feet running from the front porch to the road to meet me on summer evenings were reminders of the importance of maintaining that tradition. Seventy-five cents was designated to cover school cafeteria lunches the following week, and the remainder went into a savings account at the First National Bank of Pontotoc. The savings and interest income grew sufficiently to cover the cost of a dress and heels to wear to my eighth grade graduation.

In Uncle Lowell's drugstore, white customers had the option of being served at the old-fashioned mahogany counter or at one of the small marble-topped tables, seated on tiny round-bottomed chairs with arched backs, as they enjoyed their fountain Cokes, Coke floats, milkshakes, malts, limeades, banana splits, and ice cream sodas. Uncle Lowell had a firm rule that "coloreds" were to be served ice cream cones at the front of the store. Because disposable cups and bowls were not yet available, African American customers could not enjoy a strawberry soda, a chocolate sundae, or any treat that required a container. Having placed their orders, colored customers waited at the front door for us to return with their ice cream cones. That is, until one Saturday afternoon when an African American man who was unmindful of or dissatisfied with that convention came to the soda fountain, sat down on a swivel stool, and ordered a double dip of vanilla ice cream.

Scouring the store for Uncle Lowell, I realized he was nowhere in sight. My heart raced as I struggled with the course of action I should take, knowing without any doubt that Uncle Lowell would be incensed if I served the man at the counter. On the other hand, this was a man, albeit a dark one, and all my life I had been taught to respect my elders. After an agonizing moment of uncertainty, I loaded the cone with two exceptionally large scoops of vanilla ice cream and handed it to the man. As I took the two nickels from his pink palm, I fervently prayed that Uncle Lowell would stay away until this customer had finished eating his ice cream and departed. We were not that lucky. The man had savored only a couple of large bites of the frozen delight when Uncle Lowell's tall, lanky frame came sailing through the front door of the drugstore, not stopping until he reached the soda fountain. In one fell swoop, he took the gentleman by one arm, put the ice cream in his other hand, and escorted them both out the front door. Once they were on the sidewalk, he returned the ice cream to its owner with an admonition that all future sales were to be transacted at the front of the store.

When Uncle Lowell returned to the counter, he interrogated me about why I had broken his rule and served a colored person at the counter. Deciding it was better to be considered a little slow than disobedient, I acted dense. Uncle Lowell dropped a peg in my eyes that day. In retrospect, I realize that although he likely was expressing his own prejudice, I did not take into account that most of his white customers would have stopped frequenting Uncle Lowell's establishment had they been expected to eat or drink while seated beside a person of color.

Black people were not the only alien beings of my youth. When I graduated as valedictorian from high school, Uncle Lowell called to let me know he was willing to pay for me to attend a six-month secretarial school in Memphis if I lived with James and Marie while completing the required classes. In those days, that was a most generous offer, since girls in our area rarely attended college, and finishing a secretarial course at a reputable institution gave you a leg-up in competing for a coveted office job. I thanked Uncle Lowell but explained to him I had already taken typing, shorthand, and bookkeeping classes in high school and that my goal was to attend Itawamba Junior

College that fall and to ultimately earn a bachelor's degree in Nursing. In the mid-sixties, women in our vicinity became factory workers, secretaries, teachers, or nurses, and I had eliminated all but the latter from my list of desired professions.

My response must have seemed ungrateful, and it left Uncle Lowell a bit incredulous, unaccustomed as he was to having his offers of financial assistance rejected. However, my refusal of his gift was not the primary source of his consternation. He advised me that girls had no need for college degrees, and that to acquire one would be wasting my time and his money. He would have no part of such foolishness, and I would be wise to take some classes that would help me get a job in an office. It turns out he was at least partially correct, because during the ensuing years filled with day jobs and night classes, I might have landed better positions and earned more money had I taken him up on his offer. Being intent upon getting a degree, I told Uncle Lowell I appreciated his concern, but that my mind was made up. To someone like Uncle Lowell born in rural Mississippi in 1914, *I* was another alien being.

Uncle Lowell and his peers were part of the great generation of men that proudly fought in World War II to save the world from the tyranny, oppression, and genocide of a racist zealot. When faced with the issue of whether to allow a misguided dictator to take away the rights of human beings, including the right to life, the men of that generation chose to sacrifice their own lives for the sake of others. Yet the obstacles to freedom facing people of color and women in their own country did not seem unjust to many of them. The majority of them were good men, not monsters or even mean-spirited. Perhaps they had simply not been awakened to the oppression they perpetuated. Before *we* judge *them* as alien beings, we would be better served to question in what ways we who consider ourselves more enlightened continue to oppress or to tolerate the oppression of others.

The South of my youth is gone, both the good and the bad. Only the fervent allegiance to God and country is unchanged. The South has made massive progress in matters involving race and gender. As in other parts of the country, African Americans and women face significantly fewer obstacles in the New South. On this day in 2008, the progress that has been made is particularly apparent. Fifty years ago, who could have imagined that today, voters in Mississippi would be going to the polls to cast ballots in a Democratic Presidential Primary in which the only choices on the ballot are an African American man and a Caucasian woman? Today, the question is not whether people of color and whites should share common bathrooms and bar stools, or whether a woman is wasting time and money by pursuing a degree, but rather which of these two capable people can best lead our country as president. An African American man and a woman. *Alien beings both.*

EPILOGUE

A phrase used back home when pondering the status of a person who has not been heard from for a long time is "Whatever became of him?" Mother is rightly or wrongly proud of her children and is adamant that I include an update revealing "what became of" each of us. Likewise, the reader may wonder about neighbors and friends mentioned in these stories. Here is what I know about the people represented in these stories.

Mother's children remain emotionally close and make it a point to be there for each other when needed. Our most striking commonalities include a strong commitment to family and our ironclad will to fulfill our responsibility to our children. Physical distance has not changed our affinity for one another, nor have our differences. Politically, some of us are Democrats and others Republicans. Spirituality is a priority for each of us, though we do not all embrace the same theology. At family gatherings, we argue about politics, but in keeping with Papa's advice not to quarrel about the Bible, we steer away from the topic of religion.

We also differ in our assessment of our father. Every child grows up in a different family, and each one experiences his parents differently. Our family is no exception. Daddy played a larger role in our family during Ann, Bobby, James, and Larry's formative years. He took Bobby under his wing to help him become apprenticed in the sheet metal trade, and subsequently, Bobby assisted James in achieving that goal. Bobby believes the major injuries our father sustained when he was struck by a drunk driver changed him, rendering him physically less capable of providing for his family. The siblings who experienced Daddy in a more positive way can be more generous in their assessment of him than those of us who primarily remember our father's abandonment.

Ann became a business manager for WREC Radio and WREG TV in Memphis. She was married to Harvey for more than thirty years before his death when they were both in their mid-fifties. She now resides quite contentedly with her Doberman pinscher as her closest companion. Her yard, containing almost every species of plant native to the South, reflects her official designation as a master gardener. Ann and Harvey reared two sons together, Allen and Chris. She, her children, and their families live in the Memphis area.

For almost forty years, Bobby has owned his own business, General Heating & Cooling Inc., located in the Memphis vicinity, which has grown into a successful

HVAC company with commercial customers in several Southeastern states. He and his second wife and business partner, Loretta, call Tennessee home but spend weekends and every other spare moment on their well-appointed, four-hundred-acre ranch in Arkansas. Bobby served as mayor of Bartlett, Tennessee's ninth largest city, for sixteen years, and a street is named Flaherty Place in his honor. His one son, Jeff, and his family reside in a Memphis suburb.

Until he retired a few years ago, James managed the sheet metal division of Walker J. Walker, one of the largest HVAC companies in the Southeast. He and Marie, his wife of almost fifty years, raised a son, Greg, and a daughter, Lisa, in the small north Mississippi town of Nesbit. They recently purchased a stately nineteen twenties home in Pontotoc, and enhancing it has become one of their two shared passions. Their other passion and primary focus is playing a significant role in the lives of their four grandchildren. Marie continues to work as the business manager for a physicians' practice in Memphis, and James cultivates vegetable gardens that Mama would consider worthy of praise. While all of us appreciate dry and sarcastic wit, James inherited the ability to deliver his quips in a way that makes us laugh even on our worst days.

Larry lives in Fort Scott, Kansas, where he resided with his wife, Connie, until her death in 2008. During his adulthood, he has supported himself at various times as a portrait artist, carpenter, designer of yacht furniture, custom cabinet maker, and through other crafts. He has one daughter, Christi, and three sons, Kevin, Jonathan, and Aaron, as well as a large community of deaf and hearing friends. The one sibling who lived most of his childhood apart from the rest of the family, Larry continues to visit us sporadically. We stay in contact with him through letters and special telephone assistance provided for the deaf. The infrequent occasions when Larry's smiling face and joyful spirit appear at family gatherings are special to us.

Dianne (Dena) managed a hotel in Hot Springs, Arkansas, for several years and was subsequently a member of the management team for a conference center in North Mississippi. She now enjoys working in a less stressful role at the North Mississippi Welcome Center just outside Memphis, where she will greet you if you stop by when traveling down Highway 55. That is, unless she is in Long Beach, California, where her son and daughter-in-law, Kevin and Sujata, and her soon-to-be first grandchild, reside. Dena reared her only child in midtown Memphis very near the guesthouse she and I rented in the late six-ties, but now resides just south of the Tennessee line. The two of us remain intertwined.

After a series of management jobs in various industries, Betty Jo (BJ) returned to school and became a nurse, the profession for which she was always destined. Her jovial nature and dry humor brightened the days of her patients at the North Mississippi Medical Center until 2009, when end stage renal failure made it impossible for her to con-tinue to work. Now, she keeps her local bookstores in business through her numerous purchases, and she grows watermelons that would make Papa proud. She lives in Tupelo, and continues to enhance the lives of her family, friends, and her roommates, Gaye and Kaleb.

Tony spent a number of years as a recovering addict and active member of Narcotics Anonymous(NA) before dying at forty-five from complications associated with liver failure brought on by Hepatitis C, likely contracted during his years of drug use. Through NA, he helped many other addicts in recovery. A jack of all trades, he supported himself and his daughter, Heather, through a number of different trades, including crew member on a riverboat, auto trader, mechanic, carpenter, builder, landscaper, and groundskeeper. He ultimately supplemented his income as a photographer of auto racing. Many of his photos appeared in national racing magazines.

Cindy became a nurse at an early age and was subsequently certified as a registered polysomnagraphic technologist. She apparently is as gifted at monitoring people while they sleep as she is at keeping them awake, mesmerized by her flamboyant personality. She eventually tired of working through the night while others slept, and she returned to the field of nursing. Cindy is the most liberal of us and serves on the Mississippi Board of Directors of the American Civil Liberties Union and is involved in the NAACP. She is also the most prolific of her siblings, with six children. Johnny, Roy Jr., Robert, Stephanie, Gene, and Lowell. Cindy resides in Okolona, Mississippi.

Although Mother has a number of health issues, she is still very much with us as she approaches ninety years of age. She remains the matriarch of our family and the cog that holds us together. She continues to be a masterful Southern cook, gardener, homemaker, and a wise and adamant advisor to her children and grandchildren. BJ's and James' proximity to Mother allow them to check in on her several times a week, and most of us talk to her by phone every day and visit her often. Cindy's son, Robert, lived with Mother throughout his college years, and his sister Stephanie took his place when he graduated. Mother and our niece laughingly refer to one another as roommates. We all cherish our Mother's presence.

Mama remained a blessing and inspiration to her family throughout her one hundred and one years of life. Papa went home to his Lord when he was seventy-eight years of age, his life claimed by pancreatic cancer. Aunt Lynda Merle died in her late seventies, and in keeping with our family's longevity, Uncle Lowell lived ten years after her death. His blindness during the last ten years of his life somewhat curtained his activities, but he remained an active member of the Board of Directors of the First National Bank of Pontotoc until he died at age ninety. In spite of his earlier prejudices, he took great pride in his nieces' professional accomplishments. Aunt Louella lost Uncle Sam about ten years ago, but at ninety-four she remains as fit as a fiddle, maintaining a large yard and flower garden. Until recently, she arranged flowers from her yard to grace the altar on Sundays at the First Baptist Church of Pontotoc. Her driving style has not slowed down one whit, as evidenced by a recent traffic warning for speeding. Her son, Phillip, and daughter, Phyllis, live in other states but spend a great deal of time with her.

Mammaw was ninety-five when her gentle spirit flew up to heaven. Aunt Carrie and Uncle Howard remained two of my favorite relatives until they passed away in their eighties. They seemed thrilled each time we visited them and always had some humorous remembrance to share from our days together in the cotton patch. It is heartwarming to know they cherished us and the time we spent together. Aunt Zettie Mae was also in her eighties when she passed away. She was a talented homemaker, gardener and cook, but like our mother, her primary focus was her children and grandchildren.

Even after her parents' death, Sarah lived on in the family home until she died. Though she never married or lived with him, she and Travis courted for as long as we resided across the road from her. She became a talented seamstress and made my first wedding dress and veil. Her sunny disposition remained intact throughout our association.

Fate was not kind to Lonnie Wayne, and he was not given the opportunity to have the happy life he so richly deserved. He died in an automobile accident while still in his early twenties, reinforcing the adage that the good die young. Iona Jean has been deceased for a number of years, while Marlon lived to a ripe old age.

Miz Tutor is long deceased, but Billie Faye and Max live together in Pontotoc where Max earns a living utilizing his civil engineering expertise.

My friend Glenda and I stay in touch through Facebook and an occasional get-together. She completed her bachelor's degree in nursing and is a nurse in Pontotoc. Her two children and several grandchildren keep her and her husband of more than forty years busy and happy.

The last I heard, Belinda was a real estate agent. Like Tony and Lonnie Wayne, Randy died before his time.

By the time I entered college at age twenty-four, there were numerous career options from which a woman could choose. At thirty, I *finally* graduated from the University of Alabama (UA) School of Commerce and Business Administration and then earned my M.B.A. from the University of Alabama at Birmingham (UAB). After serving as vice president for Finance at UAB, I returned to the UA System as vice chancellor for Financial Affairs, the position to which twenty years prior I had served as a secretary and then fiscal analyst. I concluded my career as vice president and chief operating officer for the University of Connecticut (UConn). Between employment at the UA System and UConn, I worked for two exciting years as a consultant to Drummond Company, an Alabama based company primarily involved in coal mining, and had the privilege of spending considerable time at their Colombia, South America mining and transport operation. Armored vehicles and armed escorts were essential in Colombia at the time, and in retrospect, might also occasionally have been beneficial in university administration. In addition to my family of origin, my interesting and loving son, Jonathan Ryan, nieces and nephews whom I cherish as though they were my own, and a circle of fascinating and steadfast friends, fill my life. Dena and I remain intertwined.

Some childhood wounds never mend. But in the writing of these stories and through God's grace, I have uncovered empathy for and even forgiveness of my father. When our father died at fifty-eight, his possessions fit into a shoe box. The demons that pursued him must have been ferocious and unrelenting. The drained liquor bottles in his room confirmed the emptiness of his life. In his wallet was one school picture of each of his children, even those of us he hardly knew. Daddy died alone in a midtown Memphis boarding house a few blocks away from the place Dena and I had lived until six months prior. Somewhere along the way, empathy for the loneliness and regret he must have suffered penetrated my heart, softening the hurt and resentment. Beneath those layers, I found the love for our father that I buried long before his body was placed in the ground. There is even a layer of gratitude. While our mother and our grandparents gave us roots, our father's actions forced us to grow wings in order to survive, and he showed us that we could leave Pontotoc County if our dreams led us somewhere else.

It turns out Mama was right: you really cannot make a silk purse out of a sow's ear. But you can make lemonade from lemons, and that is what our family did. There are those who have faced greater obstacles than ours and attained greater success, and there are those with fewer challenges who achieved less. Some say it is how far you travel in life from where you start that matters most. Some say it is where you end up. I believe it is how you make the journey. Paramount is the companions who travel with you, through good times and bad. With their love and support, a healthy dose of tenacity, and a modicum of faith, you can overcome significant setbacks and find joy in the process. Along the way, you may even discover a forgotten "hallelujah", albeit an anguished one, lurking in your chest just waiting to be exhaled. Then you'll know that you are truly blessed.